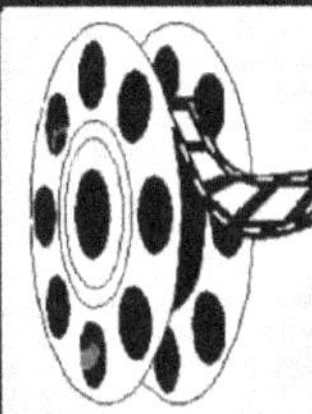

MEMBERSHIP CARD

EMPLOYEE PICKS
1428 Quick Hill Rd
Carpenter, IL 04401
(666)555-HELL

Name: ___________________________   Auth# _666_________

Signature: ________________________________

Table of Contents

The Sleepover I.................................1

The Bone Box................................10

The Sleepover II...........................36

The Dinner Party.......................44

The Sleepover III 73

who am i 80

The Sleepover IV 125

Final Girl 132

The Sleepover V 176

WALLEN COCHRANE BROWN ABELL

EMPLOYEE PICKS

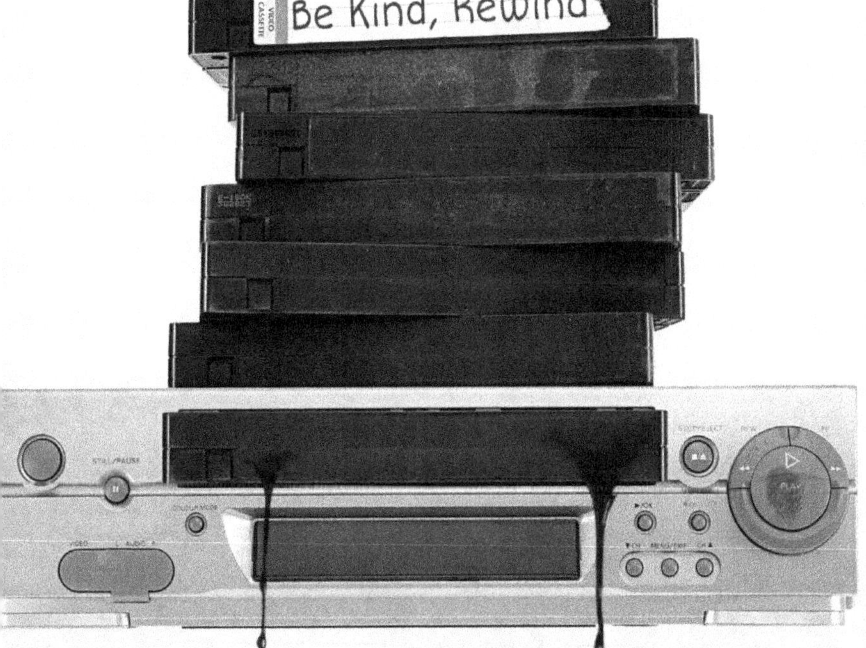

Employee Picks

By:

Sean Cochrane

Jack Wallen

Brent Abell

Dillon Brown

The Sleepover I

"Has this place always been here?" Sean asked. He stopped walking and tried to peek inside the video store's window. A thick build-up of dust and grime made it impossible to get a look inside the store.

"Dude, I can't believe we never noticed it before," Brent added. He rubbed at the dirt next to Sean with his arm, but it didn't make a difference. The filthy window wasn't coming clean.

Dillon and Jack stood behind the other two and exchanged weary glances.

"Can we get going? It's almost dark, and I bet Sean's mom will have the pizza waiting on us," Dillon said. He paced back and forth, growing anxious.

Jack crept up behind Sean and Brent. Laughing, he pushed both of them into the glass window. Sean spun around and cocked his fist back. Brent laughed, and he pointed to the poster at the top of the window. It showed four skeletons around a television set. Pizza boxes and empty soda cans surrounded them, and blood poured out of the television.

"That movie looks fucking terrible, man," Brent said.

"I don't know, I'd watch it," Dillon added.

Sean punched Dillon on the shoulder. "Bitch, you'd watch any horror flick."

"Problem with that?" Dillon asked and punched Sean back on his shoulder.

"Can we just go in and get some movies? It's getting dark, and I'm hungry," Jack pleaded.

"I'm hungry for your mom," Brent teased. Jack shook his head and opened the door to the video store and entered.

Inside, the lights buzzed and flickered. Cobwebs and dust covered everything, and Jack sneezed, looking at the shelves of VHS boxes lining the walls. Above the racks, tattered posters from old horror films covered every available space. Brent, Sean, and Dillon finally stepped inside, and stood in awe of the movie displays.

"I think this whole place is nothing but horror movies," Sean said. His mouth hung open, and his eyes opened wider than he thought possible to take in the movie collection.

"This is the best place ever," Dillon said before darting over to look at the movie selection.

"I still don't get it; how have we never noticed this place before," Brent wondered aloud.

"Who fucking cares?" Sean shot back and joined Dillon roaming the vast amount of movies.

Jack looked at the rack closest to him and cocked his head sideways. He picked up a tape and read the back description before putting it back down. "I haven't heard of any of these movies. I mean, we watch a lot of shit, and I can't say I've ever heard of these."

"Great! It's more stuff for us to watch!" Dillon called out. He looked like he was about to start dancing around the video store.

"It's pretty dirty. Don't you think if a new place opened up, it'd look new and clean?" Brent questioned.

"Fuck, dude, stop being such a downer," Sean said. He went back to perusing the movies. Sean felt overwhelmed by the amount of films he'd never heard of before.

A chilling rush of air blew through the store, and someone cleared their throat from behind the counter. All four boys froze and turned their heads to the front of the store. Behind the register stood a tall man dressed in a black *Helloween* t-shirt. He had a long black goatee, and his matching black hair was tied in a long ponytail going halfway down his back. The man's face appeared pale and gaunt, but the flickering lights made it hard to tell.

"See anything you'd like to rent?" the man asked. His voice sounded rough and gravelly.

Jack shivered. Something about the voice sounded like multiple people speaking at once, and it freaked Jack out. He looked at Sean, Brent, and Dillon, realizing they must have felt the same thing. They'd also froze and stared at the man behind the counter.

"How long has this place been here?" Brent asked. He knew they all wanted to hear the answer. The video store was the answer to their prayers. All the other places in town didn't have much of a horror section, and they'd watched every tape multiple times.

They grew bored with most of them, which they felt was a crime. How could they get bored with horror movies?

"I opened up tonight. You are my first customers for this place," the man answered. A broad grin crept across his face.

"Holy shit, did you not think to clean this place up before opening?" Dillon asked.

Sean elbowed Dillon and shot him an angry face. "Dude, shut the fuck up!"

"No, it's okay. I didn't clean it because I think it adds to the ambiance, don't you think?"

"Yeah, I'll give you that," Jack muttered.

"Ha, where are my manners? I'm Dante, and welcome to Employee Picks!"

"That's an odd fucking name," Brent said.

Dante smiled. Brent looked at him, and Dante's eyes shimmered in the light.

"Is it an odd name?" Dante asked.

The boys stood in silence. A pall washed over them, and they didn't feel right about the store anymore. Jack made a few steps toward the door, and Dante stepped out from behind the counter. Jack stopped, not knowing if Dante would try to stop him or what the clerk intended to do.

"I try to pick out movies I think my customers would enjoy and would scare the shit out of them," Dante said from the other side of the store. Jack looked back and forth from the counter to Dante. He never saw the clerk move, but he crossed the store in the blink of an eye. Jack shivered and tried to focus on the odd clerk.

"How do you know what will scare me?" Dillon asked.

"I know you're afraid of the woods. You think something out there will eat you," Dante whispered in Dillon's ear. Nobody saw Dante move, but he appeared behind Dillon. The clerk put his hand on Dillon's shoulder, and he felt his skin crawl.

"You're full of shit. Dude, you don't know me," Dillon retorted, trying to sound macho. Inside, he was scared shitless. Dillon's fear of the woods was something the rest of the guys didn't even know about, so how did the clerk know.

Dillon turned around, and Dante wasn't behind him any longer. The lights flickered, and a shadow crossed the video store. Brent screamed and almost peed a little when he felt a stale hot breath on the back of his neck. The hairs on his body all stood straight up, and goose pimples covered his arms. The breath smelled of death. He knew what death smelled like when he found his dog by the creek a few years ago. The dog's body had decayed enough he wouldn't have known it was Chester if it wasn't for his tags.

"Chester misses you, Brent."

"How did you know my name or my dog's name?" Brent asked. His voice quivered, betraying the brave front he tried to put up.

"I always make sure I know as much as I can about a town before I open a new Employee Picks location. I like to really know my clientele," Dante explained. He was behind the counter again, and a stack of VHS tapes sat next to the register.

"How did you do that?" Sean wondered aloud. His head scanned the store, and he couldn't figure out how the clerk could move so fast.

"Do what? Do my job? It's my business to know what scares people and hook them up with films that'll jolt them to their core," Dante responded.

"Hey, we saw *Aliens*," Jack said.

"Dude, that's not horror," Brent added.

"What about *Jason Lives*?" Dillon asked.

The boys started throwing out all the horror movies they'd snuck into the theater to watch over the year. The four of them believed 1986 to be the best year for horror in ages. Not that they had much experience, but they liked to discuss the films and the scene like they'd been around it for ages instead of a few years.

Dante shoved the pile of tapes to the counter's edge and smiled. Something in the clerk's grin set off alarm bells in Brent's head, but he pushed it aside.

"Do we need a membership to rent these?" Jack questioned. He knew they weren't old enough to get to a membership without their parents being there, so he knew the question was a moot point.

"Nope, the first taste is free," Dante replied. He licked his lips, and Sean swore his tongue looked pointed.

"Nothing's free," Dillon pointed out.

"These are on the house. When you bring them back, be sure to tell all your friends about my store, and we'll call it even," Dante explained.

Sean timidly took the stack of tapes from the counter. He read all the titles and realized he'd never heard of any of them. The box's backs didn't offer much information either. None of the actors or directors were familiar to him.

"Where did these come from? I haven't heard of any of these movies or people who made them," Sean stated.

Dante laughed. The laugh sounded like a howling winter wind, and the temperature in the video store fell again. "These are underground flicks. Let's say they were made for a specific audience in mind."

"So, we take these and watch them for free, and all we have to do to tell other people about this place?" Dillon asked.

"Nothing more or nothing less," Dante replied.

Brent took the tapes from Sean's hands and looked them over. Once he was done, he handed them to Jack, who gave them to Dillon. Something about the films brought a sense of impending dread with each of them. The boys looked back and forth to each other, trying to figure the catch out.

"I assure you, there is no catch," Dante said. His eyes flashed silver in the dimming lights.

"Thanks, sir, but we need to get going," Brent said.

"Yeah, we're late," Jack added.

"Well, take those home and watch them tonight. When you bring them back, we'll see what else I have for you," Dante said.

Without another word, the boys filed out of Employee Picks and back out onto the sidewalk.

"Well, that was fucking weird," Dillon said.

"I still don't understand how we've missed this place before now. We pass this spot every day on the way to school, and fuck if I've noticed it," Sean said.

"Let's just hurry up and get to Sean's so we can order pizza. We have a long night of movies to watch ahead of us," Jack stated.

Brent took the movies from Dillon and shuffled through them until he found one called *The Bone Box*. The cover looked like an animal skeleton, and he immediately thought about Chester and what Dante told him. The back description gave him a chill, and he followed along with the others to Sean's house.

He knew it was the movie they had to watch first, and the idea of watching it tonight filled him with an uneasy feeling of horror he'd never felt before.

It was going to be a long night.

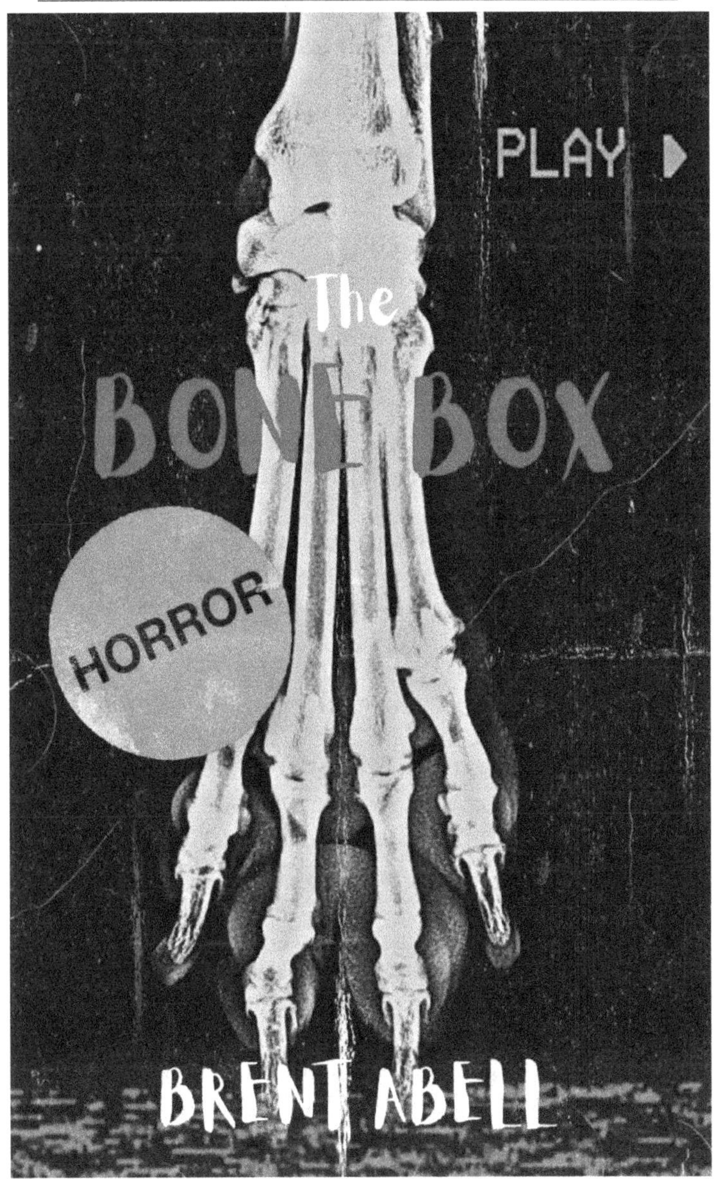
The
BONE BOX
PLAY ▶
HORROR
BRENT ABELL

The Bone Box

By Brent Abell

1

"Hey, assholes! Have you guys ever seen a dead animal before?" Andy Clarke yelled before reaching his circle of friends. He brought his bike to a screeching halt. Ryan Walters and Larry Freeman turned away from the gravel and dust, flying at them from Andy's skid. The dust covered them, and Larry growled as he brushed it off his arm.

"You fuck rag; you could've run over the baseball cards!" Ryan yelled. He shot up from the ground, his face a bright shade of angry red. Ryan wiped the dust from his glasses and leered at Andy.

Joe Cline remained seated, flipping through his cards over and over. He glanced up at the commotion and, shaking his head, went back to working on his trade proposals for the next round of offers. The boys liked pretending to be baseball team executives when they traded for new player cards.

"What the hell are you talking about, Andy? A dead animal?" Ryan asked. Larry crossed his arms and stood silently behind Ryan. Ryan knew Larry was pissed.

Andy got off his bike and let it drop to the ground next to the other bikes. "It's fucking amazing! I was biking over here, and I smelled something awful next to Pigeon Creek. I stopped to check it out, and I guess a dog got hit by a car or something because a dead one was in the tall grass along the bank."

"You showered me in dust and rocks over a dead fucking dog? I hate you sometimes," Larry said, breaking his silence.

"So, what's the big deal about it?" Joe added. He collected up his cards and put them back in the old cigar box he carried them around in.

"I think it has been there for a while. Half of its fur is gone, and maggots are crawling over it. Man, it's so cool! Come on; I want to show you guys!" Andy excitedly said, climbing back on his bike. He checked the straps holding a toolbox in place and peddled off as fast as he could.

Ryan, Larry, and Joe got on their bikes and tried to keep up with Andy. He darted back down the road like a bat of hell. Larry dropped to the back of the pack, and the others heard him cussing Andy the whole way to the corpse.

"This had better be good, bitch!" Larry called out from the rear.

The friends peddled down the dusty gravel road and crossed the old wooden bridge over Pigeon Creek. Once you crossed the bridge, the town was only a few minutes away. The summer was winding down, and soon, they'd be back to school, entering high school. Chasing Andy to see a dead dog wasn't how Ryan wanted to end his vacation. Instead, he wanted to try to hook up with Amy Brandt, but his friends weren't letting him out of their sight so he could pursue a romantic endeavor. He wouldn't trade his friends for the world, but they could be pains sometimes.

Andy slammed his brakes and jumped off his bike. The bike fell into the tall weeds between the road and creek, and Andy ran down the embankment with a rusty red toolbox in tow. The others arrived, and after dropping their bikes, they followed Andy down to the water's edge. Andy stopped long enough to turn around and wave to the others.

"Hurry up, slowpokes!"

The other three rushed to meet him. The tall weeds slapped their bare legs, and the dry brush crunched beneath their feet. The closer they got to Andy, the worse the stench of rot and decay became, filling their nostrils. Ryan gagged as bile rose in the back of his throat. Larry doubled over to vomit on the ground. Joe pulled his shirt up over his nose to block the smell wafting off the corpse in the hot summer air.

"I can't believe you pussies can't take a little bit of a bad smell," Andy taunted them.

"I can't believe you're getting all hard and heavy over this," Larry shot back. He doubled over, panting from sprinting to catch up to Andy. Running wasn't something Larry did well or often.

"Okay, asshole, what's the big deal, besides the smell?" Ryan asked.

Andy didn't reply to anything his friends said. Instead, he pulled a key from his pocket and unlocked the box's lid. He opened the rusted metal toolbox and removed a small pair of pruning shears. The dead dog's body wasn't a fresh kill, and the fur and skin were in various stages of deterioration. Andy poked it with the blades and sighed.

Joe walked up behind them, sighing heavily. "What's in the box, Andy?"

"You sound like Brad Pitt in that one movie," Ryan snorted.

Andy stopped poking at the corpse and looked up at the others. Ryan noticed the vacant look in his eyes and shuddered. Andy always seemed like an odd kid, but the expression on his face at that moment chilled Ryan.

Andy gently sat the shears in the grass and reached into the toolbox. He tilted his head to the side and instead turned the box around. Larry lowered his head while Ryan and Joe stared at the contents with a morbid curiosity.

"This is my bone box," Andy said proudly.

"No shit," Ryan said. He studied the various bones housed within the toolbox tray and felt sick to his stomach.

"I don't have a dog paw yet, so I'm going to add one to my collection now," Andy explained.

"What the fuck, dude? Why would you collect that stuff?" Larry asked.

"I like them, and they don't pick on me or make me feel bad," Andy said with a sigh. Ryan heard the hurt in his voice. They gave him a hard time from time to time, but they were friends, and that's what friends did.

At least Ryan hoped so.

"Like, do you talk to them?" Joe questioned.

Andy's face lit up like a Christmas tree, and a broad smile grew across his face. "Oh, I play with them too. They're like pets."

A knot formed in Ryan's stomach. "Man, that's pretty fucked up."

Andy knelt beside the dog and closed the shear's blades around the dog's front right paw. Maggots crawled in and out of holes in the rotting flesh, and Andy brushed them aside. His fingers felt around the foot, and he put the shears in place. Andy squeezed with all his might until the bone finally broke from the pressure, and the paw came free of the leg. A thin piece of skin and hair kept it attached, but Andy tugged on it until the paw ripped free.

"This is like the best piece in my collection!" Andy boasted.

"How big is your collection?" Joe inquired.

"I have quite a few nice animals in it. You guys want to come over and see it sometime?" Andy excitedly exclaimed.

"You can't be serious," Larry flatly stated.

Andy placed the paw and the shears in the box and closed the lid. Flecks of rust and paint fell off into the grass. Ryan wondered if the red was paint and not blood instead. For the first time, Ryan noticed skull stickers adorning the top of the box, and gray duct tape held the broken black handle together.

He reached over and pulled the box closer to him. A cloud of rancid putrid air hit him in the face when his face got close to the collection. He cringed from the pungent aroma wafting out of the box.

Larry and Joe stood behind Ryan and peeked over his shoulder at the collection. Larry screamed, and Joe dropped to his knees. Neither of them wanted to look in the box, but curiosity got the better of them in the end. Bones littered the insides. Little skeletal paws, tails, and heads filled the tray. The last remaining tissue clung to the bones in a last desperate attempt not to rot away. Small shreds of gray and black meat with tiny tufts of fur lined the bottom like a warm bed for the bones.

"Do you like it? I've been collecting all summer," Andy proclaimed.

"Close it now, Ryan," Larry whispered. His voice was barely audible.

"Yeah, I think I will," Ryan replied.

Andy stopped Ryan and shoved him away from the box. "Slow your roll, bro! I have to put this one in with the others first before we get out of here." Andy stood up with the box, and he hesitated for a moment. "I guess I don't have time to put the rest of the dog with the other bodies."

"Wait. What?" Larry wondered aloud.

Andy dropped the box and snapped the shears in Larry's direction. "If anyone finds out about this or my collection, these are coming to fucking cut you," Andy spat. The words flew from his mouth like venom, and they stung when they hit.

"What bodies?" Ryan asked. Andy unsettled him. Andy was the quiet one in the group and never raised his voice or cut up a dead dog in their presence before. Ryan wondered what they'd missed for the last five years of them all being best friends.

"Oh, I bury the bodies out behind the Anderson's barn. Nobody would ever think to look back there for anything," Andy said while stuffing the shears in his box and relocking the lid.

"If they're already dead, why do you care if anyone finds out?" Joe asked.

"Who said they were already dead?" Andy answered smugly, climbing back onto his bike. Without another word, he took off peddling down the road and quickly was out of sight.

Ryan, Larry, and Joe looked back and forth at each other and ran to their bikes. Mounting up, they shot off down the road after Andy, afraid of what their friend might be capable of doing. The knowing glance shared between the three implied their complicit silence to the deed and what they'd discovered about Andy. They hoped the price for their silence would be minimal.

2

Larry ate in silence at dinner. He pushed food around his plate, but nothing ever found itself in his mouth. His mother and father sat back and stared at him while they chewed their food.

"So, Larry, how was your day?" his father asked before taking a sip of his beer.

"Same old stuff. We traded cards out by Pigeon Creek, and Andy took us down to see a dead dog. You know, nothing special." Larry explained and finally took a bite of his peas.

His mother's head whipped up from her plate, and her mouth hung open in surprise. "He took you guys to see a dead dog?"

"Yeah, so?" Larry replied, shrugging his shoulders.

"It's kind of morbid, is all," his mother replied.

Larry's father sat at the end of the table, smiling. "Honey, they're boys. What they did is the kind of stuff boys their age do on summer break. They bike, they fish, and they check out dead animals, apparently. Hell, I did much worse things with my friends when I was his age. There isn't much to do in Hadley, so boys have to go outdoors and find something to do. It's perfectly natural."

"Like what kind of stuff did you and your friends do, dad?" Larry asked. His father had his undivided attention now.

"Walter!" Larry's mother exclaimed. When she raised her voice, she dropped her fork on her plate.

"Okay, I won't tell him about the cool things we did to pass the time down by the creek when I was young."

The three went back to their plates without another word. Larry relished the silence and started to eat his dinner when he heard a strange sound outside the door. It was faint, but it reminded him of an animal clawing at the storm door. The sound of the metal made his teeth hurt, and it raised goosebumps on his arms. Larry stared at the door with his mouth agape, a trickle of fried chicken grease dribbling down his chin. He desperately wanted to hide and read one of his new Star Wars comics, but he found himself frozen in place.

"Larry, honey? Larry, what's wrong?" his mother asked in between bites of her chicken leg.

Larry snapped his head around to his mother. "Don't you hear something scratching at the door?"

"No, son, I don't hear anything. Are you feeling okay?" Walter asked. He reached over and felt Larry's forehead.

Larry shook his head. "No, I'm fine. Can I be excused?"

"That's fine, dear. Why don't you go lay down and relax. Maybe you were out in the sun too long this afternoon," his mother said.

Larry got up from the table and left the kitchen to go to his room. On his way to his bedroom, Larry thought he heard something tracking his movements outside the house. Larry picked up his pace and shut his bedroom door quickly behind him. Timidly, he pulled back his curtains and scanned the darkening yard. A chill filled him, and he closed the curtains.

Larry didn't feel safe until he climbed into bed and completely buried himself under his blankets.

***

Outside Larry's window and behind the old oak tree, tiny red orbs glowed brightly in the coming night. They sniffed the air and raced beneath the second-story window. When they were content, this boy wasn't the one they sought; they scurried off into the shadows. In the moonlit night, they continued the hunt for their missing remains.

3

Ryan sat at his desk, staring out the window, when he heard the trashcan fall over. The ash tree branches outside his window swayed in the evening breeze and scraped against the house like boney fingers. Ryan didn't think the breeze would've been enough to blow over a trashcan, but he got up to take a peek out the window anyway. Andy sat on the floor across the room, digging in his bag for his toothbrush.

"I know I packed it, Ryan. If I can't find it, can I use yours?" Andy asked.

"Shh," Ryan shushed Andy in reply.

"Well, can I?"

"Shut up; I'm listening for whatever knocked the trashcan over," Ryan said.

Andy stood up and walked toward the bathroom door. Ryan's parents were owners of lots of property in town, and Ryan had his own bathroom in the massive house. Andy stopped by the door and looked over at Ryan. Ryan hung halfway out of the open window, trying to see in the dark.

"It was probably a cat," Andy said.

"I don't know. Farmer Anderson's mutts are always digging around here. They run down from the farm and tear up all kinds of shit in our neighborhood. You'd think they'd find something to eat closer to home," Ryan said. He pulled himself back inside his room and sat in his chair.

"I hate his dogs," Andy stated with his mouth full of toothpaste.

"His dogs are horrible. If dad hadn't taken my bb gun from me last week, I'd go out there and take care of them myself. A bb right in the ass would make them think twice about digging in our trash again," Ryan said, his finger pointed out the window like a gun.

"Have you thought about using rocks? They worked good when I went after Mr. Lee's cat last winter,"

Ryan glanced back at Andy as he walked out of the bathroom and shivered. Andy sat back down on the floor and pulled the red toolbox closer to him. Andy crossed his legs and sat the box in his lap. He carefully took the key off from around his neck and unlocked the bone box. Andy's hands caressed the rusted box, and it freaked Ryan out, watching his friend touch the morbid box in such a manner. A gleam lit Andy's eyes when he opened the container and felt the bones inside.

"So, Andy, you never told me where you found all those bones," Ryan said.

"Oh, man, ever since I found my first skeleton piece, I had to find more. I couldn't sit and wait to find them, though. Do you know how hard it is to find this shit? While you guys played catch and traded ball cards, I became a hunter. I stalked and killed everything I added to my collection."

Outside, the breeze picked up, and the curtains billowed into the bedroom. Ryan thought he heard the trash cans again, the loud banging carrying on the wind. He spun around and looked out the window only to see trash blowing across the yard. Still, Ryan felt like something was watching him look out the window, and it made him shiver. A dog howled from up the street, and Ryan relaxed a little. He loved scary movies, horror novels, and writing weird tales in English class, but what he saw when he turned back to Andy chilled him to his core.

While Ryan focused his attention outside, Andy unloaded his collection from the box. Within a few minutes, Andy had laid out most of his collection and organized it by body part. The paws made up one row, spines another, and Andy started setting out the skulls when Ryan screamed.

"What haven't you ever seen any of this stuff before? Shit, they won't hurt you, Ryan, you big wuss," Andy said. He sat up, smiling at Ryan, and put the bird skull he was holding in its place with the others on the floor.

"Jesus H. Christ, will you pick that shit up before my parents come up here. I mean, how am I supposed to explain this junk to them? Do you think I can seriously explain a pile of bones on my floor?"

"They're more than just plain old bones! They are mine!" Andy wailed.

Ryan shot up from his chair and grabbed Andy's collar. Ryan pulled Andy's face so close to his, their noses touched.

"Shut the fuck up, Andy. I want you to clean up this shit now, and we're going to bed. In the morning, we'll discuss this with Larry and Joe."

"What do they have to do with this, Ryan?" Andy asked. His voice tinged with anger.

"Maybe they need to be included in the conversation about what to do with you! This, this thing you're doing with the bones isn't fucking right. In fact, it's pretty fucking sick," Ryan replied. Anger rose in his voice also. Both boys glared at each other and balled up their fists.

"You guys don't own me," Andy whispered.

"But, we're responsible for you as your friends," Ryan whispered back before letting Andy go.

Andy sat back on the floor and didn't move. Finally, he slowly picked up his bone collection and gently placed them back in the toolbox.

"I thought you guys liked me," Andy muttered. The tough-guy bravado drained away with each bone he returned to the box.

Ryan sighed. "Andy, we do like you. I want to see what we can help you with without any of our parents finding out. Christ, they'd have you committed if they found this shit out. If the rest of our parents found out, we'd all be hanging beside you, man."

"I understand; let's go to bed and get with the others in the morning like you said," Andy said as he closed the box's lid and locked it.

Ryan turned off the light and crawled into his bed. He made sure he stayed awake long enough to hear Andy snore from his sleeping bag on the floor. Something in Ryan didn't trust his friend any longer, and he was afraid of him now.

***

St. Thomas Catholic Church's bell tolled out its midnight call, and Ryan awoke in a cold sweat. He rapidly ran his hands up and down his legs and arms attempting to warm them back up again. His skin crawled, and he felt his chest and head. Ryan let out a relieved sigh when he didn't feel anything on him, and some warmth returned to his limbs. Satisfied there wasn't anything on him, he closed his eyes and drifted back toward sleep. Ryan hovered on the fragile edge between the waking world and the dream world when he heard a clicking sound from his room's dark corner. Slowly, he opened his eyes and listened for the sound again. By his clothes hamper, he could hear something faintly tapping on his hardwood floor in the corner. The closet door creaked open, and something hard hit the floor. Ryan held his breath. The noise came closer, moving slowly through his room, hiding in the shadows. Ryan pulled the covers up over his head and prayed. His parents were devout Catholics and always tried to get Ryan to be active in the church. At his age, he'd already become jaded about religion and tended to go to mass only to appease his mother. He knew, secretly, his father didn't care either, so he didn't give Jesus much thought. Tonight, he found religion the old-fashioned way; by needing divine intervention.

In the dark, the sound came closer and closer to where Ryan hid under his blankets. He dared to take a peek and saw Andy's shape in the darkness, still curled up on the floor in his sleeping bag. Closer and closer, the sound came to his bed. Ryan clutched the blanket's edge tighter until his knuckles turned white. When something slammed into Ryan's bed, he screamed a shrill cry. Ryan reached over the threshold of his covers and turned on his lamp. When he looked down, he saw his bowling ball looking back up at him. Ryan chuckled and rolled over to see if he woke Andy up when he screamed.

Ryan recoiled in horror when he noticed the shape beneath the sleeping bag wasn't Andy. The sleeping bag was messy and out of sorts, and Ryan realized it made him think Andy was still asleep underneath it. Ryan gathered all the courage he could muster and climbed down from his bed. The first thing Ryan thought was Andy went to the bathroom. They drank a couple of two-liter bottles of root beer while they watched old *Twilight Zone* episodes. He took two steps toward the bathroom when his foot came down on something sharp. Ryan yelped in pain and looked down at his foot. The front half of a snake's skeleton reared back at him, ready to strike with broken fangs. Ryan stumbled back from the snake's remains, leaving bloody footprints behind him on his floor. The bone snake wriggled at Ryan, its glowing red eyes piercing the room's darkness. Ryan turned white when he scanned the rest of his room.

The open bone box was on its side, and the bones scattered the floor. Tiny paws flexed themselves, trying to move away from the box. Skulls in various sizes snapped their rotted teeth in his direction. Little red glowing eyes glared at him full of hatred and contempt. Ryan looked from side to side, trying to find where Andy went- he heard scratching noises sounded all around him. Ryan surveyed his room, and in the darkness, knew they surrounded him. A nightmare collection of dead creatures waited for him on his bedroom floor.

Ryan fumbled around on his desk and turned his lamp on. Once the light cut through the darkness, he realized Andy wasn't in the bathroom either. The door was ajar, and Ryan didn't see anything inside. Panic set in when Ryan noticed the skeletal army creeping up on him. Suddenly, he remembered the birthday present from his uncle under his bed. Closing his eyes, he reached cautiously underneath his bed and felt around until his fingers found the cold aluminum bat. Ryan gripped the handle and slowly pulled the bat from the darkness. He heard the clacking of bones but didn't move fast enough before a skeletal squirrel bit his hand. The bat dropped from his grasp, but he recovered it before the squirrel struck out at him again.

"Andy!" Ryan cried out as the lamp fell from the desk, breaking the bulb. The bedroom plunged into darkness.

"Andy?" Ryan asked in a whimper. The only answer Ryan received was the clicking bones closing in on him from all over the dark bedroom. He knew Andy wouldn't answer him, but he wondered where he'd gone to in the middle of the night.

The dead squirrel jumped on the bed and lurched toward Ryan. The bone jaws snapped, and a decayed tooth broke loose. It fell on the bed, and Ryan hurried to the edge of his bed against the wall. His grip on the bat tightened, and he drew it back over his shoulder.

"Fuck you, this is for my hand," Ryan sneered and swung the bat. The aluminum bat struck the squirrel squarely in its body, and the bones shattered. Little pieces of the skeleton flew all over the bed and floor.

Around the bed, the others stopped. Ryan looked at the little glowing eyes and pulled the bat back over his shoulder again. Outside, the moon cleared the clouds, and it lit up Ryan's room. The assembled skeletal zoo remained motionless. A mouse's body clicked to the others, and they turned away from Ryan. Without another sound, they lurched and shambled out Ryan's door and down the stairs. Once the last one cleared the doorway, Ryan let out a sigh of relief.

Tears flowed down his cheeks when he flexed his hand. The wound from where the squirrel bit him bled again, and he winced from the pain. In the moonlight, he examined the ragged wound on his hand, and Ryan seethed in anger. Andy brought this upon him, but he'd disappeared in the night, leaving him to fight off the damned creatures of his creation. Reaching for his blanket, he tore off a small piece to wrap around his hand to help stop the bleeding. He put on his shoes and climbed out of his window.

The night chilled him, but not as much as his encounter with Andy's box creatures did. Larry had to know about what happened. Ryan took his bike from the garage and tore off down the street, hoping Larry hadn't been visited by the unholy horde too.

***

Larry awoke around midnight and couldn't back to sleep, no matter how hard he tried. The noises he heard outside earlier never left his thoughts, even though he didn't hear them again before going to bed. The chilly breeze blew his drapes open, and he jumped when they knocked the water glass from his nightstand. Larry bolted upright, refusing to lay back down, fearful his body would betray him and sleep. He huddled under his quilt in the back corner of his bed with his head barely visible beneath the covers. His eyes remained wide open and scanning his room like a hawk. The room was silent. The breeze died off, and the room grew still.

Larry jumped out of his skin and out from under the covers when something struck his window. He sat frozen in fear and unable to move. Something else plunked his window, and he slowly climbed out of his bed. Out in the moonlit yard, he saw Ryan about to toss another rock at his window. Ryan dropped the rock, and Larry noticed the baseball bat in his left hand.

"What the hell, Ryan? It's after midnight."

"Something is very fucking wrong. I woke up, and Andy's bone shit was all over the floor. He wasn't anywhere around, but a skeletal fucking squirrel bit my hand. The other parts moved around the floor like they were fucking alive, man," Ryan explained.

Larry started to say something but stopped when he thought about the sounds he heard outside after supper. While his first instinct was to make fun of Ryan, he believed every word coming out of Ryan's mouth.

"Hold on; I'll be right down."

"Larry!"

"What?" Larry said, sticking his head back out of the window.

Ryan smiled. "Can you bring a guy some band-aids? This hand is still bleeding like a bitch."

Larry could tell how much pain Ryan must have been feeling from the sound of his voice through clenched teeth. When Larry disappeared back into his room, Ryan went to the porch to wait.

Larry slowly opened the door, so his parents wouldn't be altered to him, leaving the house in the middle of the night. The last time he'd done it, they used fifty rolls of toilet paper on their science teacher Mr. Cooper. They grounded him for a month and pulled him from the baseball team. Larry thought it'd been the worst summer ever.

When Larry left the house and went out on the porch, he handed Ryan two bandages and held out his air rifle. "It's the best I got."

"It'll be fine. The bones are just that, bones. When you hit them, they break apart like nothing was holding them together," Ryan explained. He took the bandages from Larry and used them on his oozing hands.

"So, what the shit is going on, Ryan?"

"I don't know exactly, but it's Andy's fault."

"Okay, so where do we start looking for him?" Larry asked.

Ryan whimpered when he tightened the bandages around his hand. "I have an idea, but we need to hurry."

"Are we grabbing Joe?" Larry wondered aloud.

"We should leave him out of this," Ryan replied.

Larry thought about it for a brief second and nodded in agreement.

"We need to get to old man Anderson's farm, like five minutes ago," Ryan said.

Both boys mounted their bikes and sped down the road to the farm.

4

The roosters patrolled the farm and prepared to call out the approaching morning when the boys arrived. The other chickens pecked along the front yard and barely acknowledged Ryan and Larry when they dropped their bikes.

"Where should we look?" Larry asked.

"Andy said something about burying the remains back behind the barn."

"The old one?" Larry asked.

Ryan scanned the farm and tried to think about precisely what Andy told him. Before the property turned into cornfields, Ryan spied a dilapidated red barn along the yard's back by the main barn. In the sparse light, he could tell the roof had caved in, and the walls leaned heavily to the right.

"Let's go," Ryan said. He walked past the pecking chickens and prayed Andy was fucking with them. The creatures he found in his room told him otherwise. He wasn't sure Andy was fine at all.

They sprinted through the yard toward the menacing structure in the shadows in front of them. It sat behind the house and beside the main barn. The summer's tall weed growth still covered the front of it, obscuring its presence on the property. Larry turned the corner first and saw what awaited them. His mouth hung open, and his blood froze in his veins. He reached out to grab Ryan's arm. Both boys stared at the horrific scene before them.

A macabre parade of skeletal remains twitched and writhed on the ground before them. The line moved slowly behind the barn and massed around a hole surrounded by freshly dug piles of earth. They moved silently past Ryan and Larry moving on like they didn't exist. Ryan brought the ball bat up to his shoulders. Ryan walked beside the bone procession and approached the hole. He signaled back to Larry to stay still and quiet.

The freshly dug hole awaited Ryan when he reached the end of the skeletal parade. Ryan brought the bat up to his shoulders and tried to hold back the scream building in his throat. He followed along the bone procession and peered down into the dark hole. When he saw what was at the bottom of the hole, his heart skipped a beat, and his breath left his body.

The skeletal procession marched past Ryan and walked off the edge into the pit.

Ryan realized it was the same hole Andy boasted about, where he said he put the animals' body parts he didn't keep for his bone collection. The bones crashed into the bottom and mingled around, trying to find the rest of their bodies. In the center was a human body. Ryan immediately recognized the pajamas. The last time he'd seen them was before he and Andy went to bed. The flesh had been picked clean from the body, and Ryan could make out small bite marks pocking the white bone. Ryan backed away and closed his eyes. No matter how hard he tried, the image of his friend wouldn't go away. He tried to forget the gruesome scene at the bottom of the hole. Each time he opened his eyes, the creatures in the open grave were still gnawing on his friend.

Ryan turned and ran.

Larry stood with his rifle pointed at the barn when Ryan came running out from behind it.

"Get your bike! Let's go, go, go!" Ryan screamed at Larry. Ryan got his bike and waited for a moment while Larry got on his before he took off toward his house. Larry peddled like the wind and tried to keep up with his friend.

Finally, Ryan stopped at the side of the road and tried to catch his breath. Larry stopped beside him, panting. "What the actual fuck, dude?"

"The bones, they were alive," Ryan managed to say in between breaths.

"Was Andy there?" Larry asked. Concern filled his voice.

"No," Ryan lied and rode off to his house.

***

The town searched for two weeks before calling the hunt for Andy Clarke off. Every inch of the town, surrounding woods, and the creek had been searched dozens of times. Ryan, Larry, and Joe became the target of multiple questions, and their stories about Andy's bizarre behavior the last day they spent with him lead the authorities to believe he'd run away from home.

The next spring, Ryan, Larry, and Joe went back to the creek and tossed some baseball cards in the water as their own memorial to Andy. After the summer ended, Ryan moved away, and the group lost contact with each other. This is the way of childhood; we live long enough to see our friends fade away and become distant memories.

Sometimes, things are better off being forgotten.

5

Ryan sat on his back porch and skimmed the newspaper. He still had a mail order subscription even after thirty years. Ryan approached his mid-forties, and he made peace with his life years ago. He lived with his regrets, but who didn't? After glossing over the lead stories, a headline beneath the fold on page one caught his eye.

Bones Found on Farm Before Auction

Ryan's heart skipped a beat. After all these years, he couldn't believe they finally found Andy's private cemetery. A smile grew across Ryan's lips, and he gently folded the paper and placed it on the small table beside his chair. He peeked in the living room window off the porch and saw his wife and two kids seated on the couch watching a movie. He moved past them and headed out to the garage.

The garage was Ryan's refuge. Inside, when work got shitty, or he had a fight with Michelle, he'd step into his two-car sanctuary to reconnect with his childhood. He'd purchased an old Mustang to rebuild, and it was the place he'd go to recharge. Ryan entered the garage and headed straight for the Mustang. The truck was opened, but he didn't mind. Neither Michelle nor the kids dared to venture out into his world. The garage and the car were the one thing they allowed him to have for his private time.

Ryan stood before the trunk and sighed. They'd finally found Andy. He never told Larry or Joe about finding the body. Instead, he quietly returned after leaving Larry at his house and filled in the grave. He checked around the property, found an old tractor tire to mask the fresh dirt piles, and hoped his friend would remain in peace forever.

They never found the bone box. Ryan made sure they never would either. He sighed and lifted the rusted red box out of the Mustang's trunk and sat it on the workbench.

"Well, old friend, I guess we may have to return home to answer some questions," Ryan solemnly said.

Tears filled Ryan's eyes as he opened the box and gazed at his own souvenir from that summer. The eyes had long decayed, and the flesh eaten from his bones, but having Andy's skull brought a sense of relief and peace to Ryan.

He only hoped nobody else ever found out about his bone box.

The Sleepover II

"Woah," Sean said, stuffing another handful of potato chips into his mouth. "That was fuckin' sweet." The boys were seated together in the living room, glued to the television as the final credits rolled.

"I'm not going to lie," Brent started. "That ending messed me up."

"Don't be a pussy," Dillon said, tossing a pillow at him, narrowly missing his head. "I mean, yeah, it was scary, but not like 'the scariest movie ever made' scary."

"Dude, I literally saw you covering your eyes for the entire ending. You didn't even see the final shot!" Jack looked at Brent and nodded, as if to say, *I got your back.*

"Whatever," Dillon said, sheepishly. "Okay fine, yeah, it was creepy."

"It was awesome," Sean said. "I want more. What should we watch next?"

Brent went to the VCR and hit Eject, but the tape wouldn't come out. He pushed the button again. Nothing.

"What the hell?" He repeatedly hit the button over and over.

"Dude, if you break that, my dad's gonna kick our asses," Sean warned.

"Don't piss off Sean's dad," Jack added. "I've been on the wrong end of that; you want to talk about something *really* scary..."

The VCR suddenly sparked and smoke billowed from it.

"Oh shit," Dillon said, jumping from the couch and rushing to Brent's side.

"Oh shit is right," Sean said, getting up. "You better not have busted this thing, man."

"I hope it didn't eat the tape," Jack said. The four boys huddled around the VCR. It sparked again, and then the tape effortlessly ejected. Brent reached out and took it out, carefully inspecting it to make sure there was no damage to it. Replacing a VHS tape would surely be expensive, and the guy who owned the place had given him the creeps. He definitely didn't want to have to tell him they'd trashed one of his tapes.

"Close one," Sean said. "But I don't know if we should try another one. What if it keeps acting screwy?"

"Oh man, don't cancel movie night," Jack pleaded. "If I go home, I'm gonna get the 'What Is This Satanic Propaganda' speech from my grandma about my Judas Priest tapes I accidentally left out. I'm already busted, but man, just let me get one more night with the boys before I'm grounded for an eternity."

"I don't want to call it a night either," Dillon said. "We have three more movies here, movies nobody has ever even heard of, and it's gonna be the world's biggest dick tease to not get to watch them."

"You gonna watch through your fingers again?" Sean said, poking him in the ribs.

"You wanna watch through a black eye?" Dillon fired back.

"I'll just carefully put the next tape in and see if it acts funky." Brent reached over and took the next tape off of the stack.

A crash upstairs startled them.

"What the hell was that?" Jack asked.

"Sounded like glass breaking," Brent said.

"Shit," Sean said. "It's my mom's damn cat. I hate that thing."

"I'll go check it out," Dillon said, standing up. "You want me to put him outside if I catch him?"

"*If* you can catch him," Sean said. "He's a biter, so watch yourself."

"So's Brent's sister, but I'm not scared of that," Dillon said, sticking out his tongue.

"I'm gonna nut-punch you as soon as you get back," Brent said.

"Don't start the next one without me!" Dillon jogged out of the room and took to the stairs, skipping each step on the way up and then standing at the top of the hall.

"Here kitty, kitty, kitty," he said. "Come here you little shit." Dillon checked the first room, Sean's bedroom, and checked for anything that would have been the source of the crash. His eyes moved around the room, passing across the movie posters for *Halloween* and *A Nightmare on Elm Street*. A Tony Dorsett jersey was tacked on the wall over his messy bed.

Another crash came from down the hall.

"What the hell is going on up there?" Sean yelled from downstairs.

"Your cat's a real dick is what's going on!" Dillon yelled back. He left Sean's room and went further down the hall, hoping to find the furry little bastard before it did anymore damage. Dillon stopped when he saw glass on the ground at the end of the hall. He looked up and noticed the upstairs window that looked out over the backyard was broken, as if a baseball had been through it. Problem was, he couldn't find any signs of something on the ground.

A flutter.

Dillon spun around at the sound, looking for any signs of movement. Nothing. He turned to his left and went in through the open door that led into Sean's parents' room. Looking around, his eyes fell on the ground by the window at the end of the room. It was broken as well. And again, nothing on the floor to indicate what exactly broke the glass.

CAW!

A crow buzzed his head, causing Dillon to drop to his knees and cover himself with his arms. The bird flew around the room, knocking a vase off of a dresser and shattering it on the floor.

"Guys! Shit! Help!"

The boys ran up the stairs, all of them shouting, and Dillon crawled out of the room, half laughing and half in disbelief.

"What the hell is going on up here?" Sean barked.

"There's a damn bird in here! It flew through the window!" Dillon got to his feet and the boys all ducked as the bird flew out of the bedroom and down the hall towards the stairs.

"Holy shit, that's awesome!" Jack cackled at the ridiculous situation. "How the hell are we going to get it out of here?"

"Does your dad have a shotgun?" Dillon asked.

"Don't even think about it," Sean hissed back. "Maybe we can trap it in a bed sheet or something."

A second bird ripped through the air above them, this one coming out of Sean's room, circling the boys, and then tearing off down the hall in the direction of the other one.

"What the fuck is happening right now?!" Sean ran back down the stairs, with the other three boys all laughing behind him. Once downstairs, they watched as the birds frantically flew around the living room, before each slamming headfirst into the wall behind the television set, leaving splatters of blood and feathers, and their lifeless bodies dropping to the ground.

"Holy shit!" Brent ran to the two corpses and knelt down to look at them. The other boys were quickly in tow.

"Why would they do that?" Jack asked, bewildered.

"Maybe because they were scared?" Dillon offered.

"Look at their eyes," Brent whispered. "Something's not right."

The birds both had white, milky eyes, that seemed void of any life. And their skulls seemed sunken in and almost dry. These birds didn't look fresh at all. They looked like they'd been dead for days. Brent reached to touch one, but Jack grabbed his arm.

"Don't," he warned. "What if they're infected with some kind of disease? My grandpa says birds carry all kinds of diseases."

"They don't look like they were just alive a minute ago," Brent said. "These birds look... old. Dead for a while."

"That's impossible," Dillon said. "I watched them fly... we all watched them fly..."

"Guys," Sean said from behind them. "What the fuck is going on here?" He was looking at the couch. The bag of potato chips was lying knocked over, a product of when they'd all rushed to the stairs at the sound of Dillon's yelling. But the chips were growing mold, and cobwebs and dust covered the coffee table, couch, and end tables. The house looked like it'd been uninhabited for months. Everything smelled old and musty.

"I want to go home," Dillon said.

"Me too," said Brent.

The VCR suddenly clicked and whirred, and they all turned around to face the TV as it crackled to live. An empty VHS box lay on the floor. Brent bent over and picked it up, just as the tracking lines started to fade and the opening credits started to play.

"Dillon," he said through frightened words, "it's your pick. *The Dinner Party*."

Dillon heard the VCR whir to life as Brent ejected his movie and then held up the next one. Looking around confused, Dillon noticed the room was back to normal: no decaying furniture, no dead birds on the ground. His friends hadn't moved from their seats.

"Dillon," Brent started, "it's your pick. *The Dinner Party*."

"Yeah, sure," Dillon said, feeling uneasy. He was positive what he'd just seen had actually happened. Was it all in his head? Was he going crazy?

"You alright dude?" Sean asked.

"Yeah," he lied. "Just play the movie."

Be Kind
Rewind
THE
DINNER
PARTY
BY DILLON BROWN
PLAY ▶

The Dinner Party

by Dillon Brown

June 12th, 1985

The first camping trip of the year was always the best.

Aaron and his girlfriend, Haley, finished loading their car with the last of the camping gear and gave each other a high-five on a job well done. Haley turned to get into the car and Aaron playfully spanked her butt, causing her to turn around and smack his arm.

"Pervert," she said, smiling at him.

"*Your* pervert," he corrected.

They were going camping with their friends: Haley's best friend Camille and her boyfriend Jackson, their mutual friend Paul, and Erica, Aaron's ex-girlfriend whom he'd stayed close with after their breakup, and especially after her brother had died in a car accident two years before, in 1983.

Haley was open to Aaron staying in contact with his ex; she wasn't the jealous type and she trusted him. But she didn't expect to be going on a camping trip with her. The thought of her and Aaron having so much history at the campground and probably having sex everywhere she looked, aggravated her a little. But, she knew this trip was going to be good for Erica, and she had been nothing but supportive and sweet to her since she'd started seeing Aaron, so she kept her thoughts buried deep down, hoping alcohol wouldn't wake them up later.

"You sure you're okay with all this?" Aaron asked, as if reading her mind. She felt a tinge of embarrassment creep up, like he knew what she was thinking about. But how could he? She'd kept her cool.

"I am," she said, half-lying. "I know she's gone through hell the last two years and I know that she really needs to be out of the house because of the whole '*death anniversary*' and everything." She really felt that way, but she was still a tad worried.

"Well, you're a wonderful human being for being so supportive and understanding," Aaron said, taking her hand and kissing it as they started the long drive up to Dingman's Lake in Northern California. The lake was a popular spot for college kids to venture to during Spring Break, because it was so far away from everything, which meant almost anything could happen without a Park Ranger ever poking around. It was also famous for the tragedy that had happened there in the early 1800's when the first settlers were heading out West in search of gold and new territory to claim.

"I try," she said, smiling.

"I just need you to know, one more time: there is nothing there for Erica. There hasn't been for a long time, and there never will be again. I'm all yours." He squeezed her hand.

"I know babe," she said. "I trust you. I've always trusted you. It's just going to take a little adjusting and I'll be fine. That place has a lot of memories for you two, so it's not like I don't have *any* reservations." The words seemed to come out before she could stop them, and she hoped it wouldn't start a fight right before their soon-to-be righteous getaway.

"We *do* have a lot of memories there," Aaron said. "But I want to make new, more important memories there with you. It's my favorite place in the entire world. Plus: we can do it in the lake, which is something I've never done and always wanted to do." He winked at her and stuck out his tongue.

"Yeah, well, we'll see about that," she said, patting him on the arm. "You can earn your way up that ladder."

***

They pulled off the highway, onto the dirt road that would take them up to Dingman's Lake. There was only so much access up there with vehicles, so they'd all have to pile into Paul's truck when he and the others got there. It would be a tight fit, but the drive wasn't long from there.

Paul wasn't far behind, and soon the group was on their way up the winding dirt road that lead to their favorite spot: a secluded area that allowed easy access down to the lake, but kept them far away from the families that frequented the lake so they could be loud, raucous and drunk the entire time they were there.

Haley rode in the backseat, sandwiched between Aaron and Camille, with Erica and Jackson sitting in the front seat and Paul driving. Camille had jumped at the opportunity to get in the back before Haley was subjected to sitting next to Erica, because even though she knew her best friend was level headed and would keep her cool, she didn't want to start the trip off more awkward than it was already going to be.

"I can't believe he invited her up," Camille had said a few days before they were going. "It's pretty bogus if you ask me."

"It's not, though," Haley said, defending Aaron. "And he didn't invite her; Paul brought it up and *your* boyfriend was also on board, because they all feel bad for her."

"They all think she looks good in a bikini," Camille said, raising an eyebrow. "I know how that girl looks. Yeah, she's pretty perfect. And it makes me sick. Plus: she's a total mall-maggot."

"Stop being a Valley girl," Haley said, half-joking. "It's not a big deal. The girl hasn't done anything to me, and she's been through some pretty awful things lately. I think Aaron still being there for her is actually pretty admirable."

"Unless he's trying to be there for her because his penis misses her," Camille said suspiciously. "But I'm not going to make a big deal about it, okay? If you say it's cool, then it's cool. But I'm gonna have my eyes on that bimbo. Believe me."

The truck pulled around a long turn and then Paul eased it off the road and into a large opening, surrounded by tall pine trees and thick manzanita brush. Below them, they could see the lake, and a trail wound its way down to it. Behind them was nothing but mountains. They couldn't see the larger campgrounds from this place, and Haley was surprised at how much Aaron's description of the place had been so spot on. It really was like stepping foot into a painting.

"Time to pitch some tents, boys," Paul said. "Oh, and also set up the tents for sleeping." He burped and laughed at his childish joke and Jackson and Aaron just waved him off. "Hey, Aaron," he said, "can I talk to you real quick?"

"Yeah dude, of course," Aaron said, walking off to the side with Paul.

"So, uh, I know it's pretty mental with your new girl and your old girl here and everything," Paul started.

"It's really not though," Aaron corrected. "It's not a big deal."

"Okay, well, that's good. Then you won't mind if I try and sleep with Erica this weekend?" He gritted his teeth and sucked in air, making a hissing sound.

"I'm going with Haley, so what Erica does is none of my business." He put his hands on Paul's shoulders. "But to be honest, dude, you're gonna need to find a magic lamp to make that wish come true." He patted Paul, who scoffed at him, and then started back towards the group to start setting up camp.

***

"So I know there's got to be a good scary story about this place," Haley said as they sat around the campfire. The boys had a pyramid of beer cans started and were already showing signs of getting to the point of not being able to walk in a straight line, and the girls were passing around a bag of cheap wine that they'd pulled out of the box.

"You gotta slap that bag before you drink," Paul instructed them, but Camille just rolled her eyes and took a long swig before closing the spout and handing it off to Erica.

"There actually is," Erica said. "I'm not good at telling stories though."

"So I guess that's my cue?" Aaron said, smiling at her. She smiled back, and Haley just laughed lightly and then took the wine from her and took a huge gulp.

"I can tell it," Jackson said, standing up and wobbling around.

"You can't even say your ABC's," Camille scolded. "Sit your ass down."

"You just got whipped, boy!" Paul said, laughing obnoxiously.

"I'm gonna drown you in the lake by the end of this weekend," Jackson said, pointing a finger in Paul's face, to which Paul swatted at, nearly falling out of his chair.

"Shut up so I can tell the story," Aaron said. "Haley, since this is your first time, you have to make the sacrifice."

"Uh, what?" Haley looked around nervously, with the group all staring at her. "Sacrifice?"

"You'll understand by the end of the story," Erica said. "Go ahead babe."

The group suddenly got quiet and all eyes were on her, and Aaron just sat silent for a moment before looking at Haley uncomfortably.

"Oh my god," Erica said, putting her hand over her mouth. "I'm so sorry. I don't know... I'm so sorry." She got up and ran from the campfire and past the tents, into the woods.

"I can break her nose for you," Camille said, standing up and looking to Haley for permission. "No way. That bimbo did *not* just say that right now."

"It's fine," Haley said. "Stop. Just, don't make a bad situation even worse. I'll go talk to her."

"Sweetheart," Aaron said, trying to stop Haley. "We can just go. This was a bad idea. I feel like a jerk."

"It's fine, you guys. Chill out. I'll go talk to her. It's not a big deal and she's obviously having a worse time than any of us right now. Just let me go check on her." Haley went into the woods after her.

"You're dating a damn saint," Camille said, looking at Aaron. "Stupid idea to bring your damn ex out here with your new girl. What a space cadet."

"Shut your ass, Camille. Jackson would have more fun here without you anyway, so you have no room to talk." Paul smiled at his comment and then looked to Jackson, who looked horrified and was trying to find any words to say.

"Oh, is that so?" Camille folded her arms and glared at her boyfriend.

"No, not even...man, fuck you!" He punched Paul in the arm as hard as he could, almost knocking him out of his chair. "You're the one who brought it up to bring her in the first place because you're trying to get at her!"

"Pervert," Camille said.

"Hey, don't blame me because she spazzed out," Paul said, slurring his words.

"Would you all just shut up? This is supposed to be a bitchin' weekend and you're already all making this the trip from hell. Just chill out and stop saying dumb shit," Aaron said, slapping Paul in the back of the head.

In the trees, past where they'd left the truck, Erica crouched beside a large pine and cried into her knees. She had never felt embarrassment like this before and she didn't know why she bothered coming on the trip. A voice called out to her.

"Erica?" It was Haley, coming through the trees and walking towards her with her hands in her pockets.

"I'm sorry," Erica said, wiping tears from her cheeks. "I don't know why I said that."

"The wine talking," Haley offered, giving a weak smile.

"Why are you so...cool?" Erica looked up at her with a solemn face. "You could have easily told them not to invite me. And now you're up here talking to me after the most embarrassing moment of my life."

"I don't have any bad feelings towards you," Haley said, kneeling down. "I'm sure by some kind of 'Current Girlfriend Code' I'm *supposed* to, but I don't." She sighed. "Aaron's a pretty good guy, isn't he?"

"He is," Erica said, hugging her knees against her chest. "He's always checked on me after the crash. I don't still *like* him, you know?"

Haley felt a sense of relief wash over her, though she wasn't sure if Erica was just telling her what she wanted to hear. Still, it was a relief.

"He's just...familiar," she continued. "To a simpler time when I still had my brother. But that's all that was back there. Just having a hard time letting go of the past."

"You never have to let go of the past," Haley said, reassuring her. "I know the circumstances. And if staying close to Aaron gives you some comfort, I'm totally okay with it. Maybe we can become friends, too."

Erica smiled at her and nodded her head.

"Thanks, Haley," she said, standing up and putting out her arms for a hug. Haley hugged her back, feeling like a weight was lifted off of both of them. She knew this girl didn't have any bad intentions; she could tell she was just trying to hold on to a bit of happiness that she had after such a horrific loss.

Caw!

A crow buzzed Haley's head, barely missing her with its clawed feet.

"Shit!" she said, ducking down. The bird circled back quickly and landed on the ground, hopping around. She could tell something was wrong with it. It's eyes weren't right... milky, lifeless, dead.

"Get out of here!" Erica tossed a rock at the bird, making it scamper off.

"What was wrong with it?" Haley asked.

"What do you mean?"

"It's eyes; they didn't look real. They were white."

"Probably just old," Erica said with a tinge of nervousness to her voice.

"Let's go back to the fire," Haley said. "Time to tell me that spooky story you all promised me."

***

The girls had come back to the fire and, despite a few cold looks from a suspicious Camille, the group of friends were having a good time passing around a bottle of Schnapps and singing loudly to Def Lepard and Mötley Crüe. Haley finally begged them to tell her the story they'd told her about.

"If you really want to know," Aaron said, smirking at her.

"I do! I love scary stories. It's the best part about camping," she said.

"I'd say sleeping bag humping is the best part, but whatever you say," Paul added, laughing.

"I think you'll be on a solo mission this trip," Camille said, sticking her tongue at him.

"Alright, alright: enough with the bullshit, let's tell this story. Who's telling it this year?" Jackson took a long swig off the bottle before passing it to Haley.

"Well, Haley is the new girl here and Aaron is her boyfriend, so I say Aaron does the honors," Paul said. The group agreed.

"Aaron has to tell it," Erica said. "You two space cadets always screw up the ending." She pointed to Paul and Jackson, who recoiled in disagreement.

"I'll tell it," Aaron said. "Pass me the bottle first." He took it and drained the last of it and then tossed it into the fire, sending embers flying into the air like an army of angry lightning bugs.

"It all started in 1846, in these very mountains. In fact, that road we drove in on? That's the old trail that was the only way in or out of here, long before there were campsites and boat docks.

"So there were these settlers, right? They were moving their way from the East Coast to help forge the way for the new World, out here in the West. Captain William Dingman led them from Missouri all the way here: sixty-four people in total. They were hoping to start a town and strike it rich with gold. But a freak storm hit, right in this very place, and trapped them. There was so much snow that they couldn't pull the wagons, and many of their cattle and horses died because they couldn't find anything to eat. The group tried to forge on, but when they found the lake – this one right here – they knew that they'd never get all the way around it alive. The snow was still coming down. Feet and feet of it.

"Well, legend has it that Dingman and some of his men shot the remaining horses to help feed the people traveling with them, but once the food ran out, he resorted to eating the next best thing: their dead. Many of the travelers had died of starvation or hypothermia, so instead of burying the bodies, they ate them to survive. But Dingman became obsessed with the taste of human flesh, and he started to have cravings that he couldn't deny. He felt like he was gaining power by consuming human meat, and he needed more. Something was causing the pit in his stomach to never fill.

"While out wandering one day, Dingman and his crew found a way out, but because of his yearning to continue eating his own people, Dingman ordered the men not to say anything, and instead they stayed here and continued shooting, stabbing, strangling his own people so he could eat them. And soon there were only members of his brigade left, and Dingman furiously had them dig in the snow for anyone left to eat. They eventually fell victim to the vicious cold, and were never found. Dingman was the last man standing, and once he was alone, the presence that had overtaken his body and caused him to grow so hungry started to change him. He grew large antlers out of his head, and his body changed into something part wilderness, part animal. The curse of the Wendigo, a Native American creature that punishes man for his crimes out here. When you're all alone in the deep, dark, wood, the Wendigo will appear and rip you to shreds.

"But the legend here says: if you come here to stay in the very place they all died, you must leave them a sacrifice of blood to sate their hunger, lest you want them to rise from their icy graves and host a dinner party with *you* as the main course. And if you listen closely, when the night is at its most still, you can hear the raspy breath of the Wendigo inhaling and exhaling, with the faint cries of its victims trapped inside of it." Aaron smiled and slapped Jackson's hand, knowing he'd told the story beautifully.

"Nobody tells it like you do," Paul said, raising a beer into the air. "But Dingman didn't turn into the Wendigo. He just joined the Wendigo's army of the undead."

"Who the hell told it like that?" Aaron asked.

"My dad," Paul said.

"I've heard it both ways," Erica said. "Some people believe the Wendigo was here long before and that Dingman's caravan is trapped under its spell, and others say Dingman turned into the creature after eating the human flesh."

"It's all stupid," Camille interjected. "Just silly stories for when we were kids."

"Legends change over time," Aaron said. "I guess the next group of kids to come up here for the first time will have their own version of it. As long as the sacrifice is made, who really cares, right?"

"Maybe the sacrifice is just part of a stupid re-telling that none of us should have believed," Camille said. The group fell silent for a moment, and Haley could tell something was chewing at them. "What?" Camille continued. "We don't know for sure if there's any merit to that stupid idea. What if... now don't get all offended that I'm messing with your precious little ghost story... but what if cutting ourselves actually makes it worse? What if the blood summons the Devil or something?" The group looked at her for a moment.

"That's ridiculous," Erica muttered.

"Well, however it's told, it doesn't matter: to Dingman!" Paul sloppily poured it into his mouth and let it run all over his face and shirt. Erica just rolled her eyes at the pig.

"It's tradition," Erica whispered in Aaron's direction.

"You said I was the 'new girl,' so I have to make the sacrifice?" Haley felt a knot in her stomach. She didn't like blood, and she definitely didn't want to spill her own for some stupid campfire tale.

"Those are the rules," Paul said.

"This is so stupid," Camille said. "No. You don't have to slice yourself up."

"Actually, she does," Jackson said. "Every one of us has done it on our first outing up here. Even you have one, Camille."

Camille looked at the thin scar that ran across the palm of her hand and closed her fist around it.

"Yeah, well, it was a stupid thing to do," Camille said. "Plus, we were thirteen years old. Nobody believes in this silly crap anymore. It's *bogus*. Don't listen to them."

Haley seemed relieved that at least she had Camille on her side, but she didn't like the way Erica was keeping her gaze focused on the fire. She seemed bothered by something. Maybe it was still the embarrassment of the events earlier. Still, something didn't feel right.

"I've had enough campfire stories," Aaron said. "Nobody has to make a blood sacrifice." He winked at Haley, and she let out a sigh of relief, which made the rest of them laugh. "It's time to drain the main vein, though." He got up and stumbled away from the fire, into the darkness. They could hear the splashing of his piss hitting the ground and Camille scoffed at it.

"Such an awful story for a place that looks so beautiful," Haley said, breaking the silence.

"The most dangerous things are always the most beautiful," Jackson added, looking at Camille and blowing her a kiss.

"That was some Grade A cheese," she said, unable to control a wide smile that spread across her face. "But I like cheese. Time to join me in the tent, spaz."

"Schweet!" Jackson jumped to his feet and slung his arm over Camille's shoulder as they made their way to the tent. "If the tent's a rockin', don't come a knockin'!" He exclaimed.

"Oh barf me out," Paul jeered back at them. "Give her one for me, though, will ya?" Paul watched them disappear inside and then looked at Erica, who was still seated near the campfire.

"So, uh, Erica," he started. "My tent's got extra room in it if you want to stay in there tonight." His voice cracked. She looked up at him and then over to Aaron, who broke her gaze quickly and looked at Haley.

"I mean, I guess...," Erica started, but Aaron cut her off.

"You can crash with Haley in our tent if you want; I can stay with Paul." He could feel Paul's glare burning through the back of his skull, but he didn't care. Erica was never comfortable around Paul, even when the two were dating, and he didn't want to subject her to his drunk advances all night inside his tent.

"It's fine," she said, surprising him, and making Paul whip his head around. "I'd like to stay with you tonight, Paul." She offered him a smile.

"Oh, wow, okay," Paul said, eyes wide with excitement. "Yeah, well, let me go grab the extra blanket from the truck and I'll see you inside." He silently mouthed 'fuck you' to

Aaron before heading off into the darkness. Erica looked at Aaron and Haley for a moment before standing up from the fire and heading into Paul's tent.

"Want to tell me what the hell *that* was all about?" Haley stood, crossing her arms and staring at Aaron, who immediately took a defensive stance.

"Haley, it's not like that," he pleaded. "I just know how Paul can be and - "

"And you didn't want him to sleep with your ex-girlfriend, who called you 'babe' earlier, and who you invited up here to come camping with us." She laughed and threw her hands up in the air. "I don't get it, Aaron. I've been more than welcoming of her being here and her current situation. I've tried to keep it cool. I don't know any other girl that would be okay with their boyfriend's ex hanging around like this. But here I am. And yet here we are: you're still acting like you two are dating. I've seen the looks at each other all night. You're obviously not ever each other."

"Now wait a minute," Aaron protested. "You were the one who insisted it was fine if she came along, even when I asked if you were sure. And you were the one who went to comfort her in the woods after she embarrassed herself."

"And *you* are the one who just proved to me that you're not ready to move on," Haley said, turning around and walking away from the fire.

"Haley, wait!" Aaron started after her, but she turned and swatted his hand away when he tried to grab her shoulder.

"Don't," she said. "Don't. I'm sleeping in Paul's car tonight." She turned and continued walking away, leaving Aaron standing there, trying to figure out what to say.

***

Paul and Erica laid next to each other, staring up at the roof of the tent, and listened awkwardly as Camille moaned out and Jackson grunted, skin slapping skin in what seemed like a never-ending sexual decathlon. Just as they heard what they thought was Jackson's climactic moment ending in a loud "ah-ah-ahhh!", the two started up again.

"Well this is extremely awkward," Paul said, trying to cut the tension. Erica laughed and agreed. "You know," he finally gathered the courage to say, "we could always give them a taste of their own medicine?" He couldn't believe he'd just said that.

"Did you really think that would work with me, Paul?" Erica sat up and looked down at him. "You've known me for a long time. Have I ever been that type of girl?"

"No," Paul said sheepishly. "I'm sorry, Erica. I don't know...I'm just drunk."

"I'll tell you what," she said, catching him off guard. "*You* convince Haley to give the blood sacrifice, and *I'll* give you a handjob.

Topless." Her stare was dead serious and Paul could feel his heartbeat start to race.

"You mean, the sacrifice from the story?"

"Yes. Like we've all done. You get her to do it, and I'll take care of that." She pointed at the bulge in his sweatpants. Paul laughed nervously and then watched as Erica pulled her shirt open and showed him her breasts. "You can taste them, too," she whispered. He licked his lips at the sight of her small, pink nipples and then she quickly closed her shirt again. "Get to it, then."

Paul grabbed a flashlight from his pack and scrambled out of the tent in search of Haley. He swung the beam of light around the campsite and jumped back in fright when Aaron appeared out of the darkness.

"Jesus!" Paul said, clutching his chest. "Yo, uh, where's Haley?"

"She's totally pissed at me," Aaron said. "She's sleeping in your car tonight. Why?"

"Uh, so, Erica propositioned me."

"Oh, this ought to be good. Spill it."

"Okay, see, if I can convince Haley to do that stupid blood sacrifice from the story, then she's gonna... *relieve me.*" He made a jerking motion with his arm and stuck his tongue out at Aaron, who shook his head in disgust.

"Good luck with that," Aaron said. "If she tells you no, which she *will*, you better leave her alone. Because if she comes back here and says you're trying to force her into it, I'm going to make sure you leave camp this weekend with a broken nose." Aaron patted

Paul on the arm and then turned and went to his tent.

"Take a chill pill, man," Paul said under his breath. He stumbled through the trees on his way to find Haley, hoping to god above that she would understand his position, make the small cut, and then he'd be laying on his back, staring up at Erica's boobs and feeling her silky smooth touch as it stroked him.

A figure stood in the trees, with its back to him. It was a girl; he could tell by the way her hair flowed down across her shoulders. She looked hunched over. He figured it was Haley, but she looked hurt, or possibly sick.

"Haley?" He called out. "What's wrong?" He approached her and placed his hand on her shoulder. It was cold and bony and the figure turned around quickly, his flashlight illuminating the face of a young woman, whose face was bloodied and wrought with frostbite and her nose was nearly decayed away, with two dark red voids of exposed cartilage pulsing and quivering as she hissed at him, opening her mouth wide, a stench of rot and death pouring from her maw, her teeth brown and blood-stained, her cheeks missing flesh and showing the tendons in her jaw as she clamped her teeth around Paul's throat, ripping flesh from his neck, pulling his trachea and larynx apart with blood exploding out of them, and greedily swallowing the wad of meat she took in her mouth.

Paul tried to scream, but his throat being torn open only allowed a wet, glottal sucking sound as the white, vacuum hose-like trachea flopped around and spewed an almost pitch black blood. Paul let out one last gasp as a spurt of blood launched from his open throat, before he dropped to his knees and collapsed in a heap on the ground.

The living corpse of a woman dropped down and began to feed, as the other members of her party started to emerge from the trees. A flock of crows sprang to life from the darkness and swarmed the body, pecking and tearing flesh off of Paul, darting between the cannibalistic settlers. They were missing feathers, with milky eyes and exposed bones. One of the settlers snatched a bird in his rotten hand and stuffed it into his mouth. It was the last thing Paul saw before his head was pulled from his body and thrown off to the side.

***

Haley heard the strange crunching sound coming from the darkness and wondered if a bear had wandered into camp and started to dig through the trash. She wasn't used to the wilderness and the thought of a wild animal this close to her was making her question her decision to storm off. She was royally pissed at Aaron, but she wanted nothing more than to be with him right now.

Deciding she would chance the darkness to go back to the others, Haley turned around and started back, trying to find her way through the trees. She could hear footsteps, as if the fellow campers had all suddenly decided to get up and walk around, and she could see figures milling about, but she couldn't make any of them out. A tall, gaunt man was wandering in her direction, and she thought maybe it was Paul, but the awful sound it was making caused her to stop walking and squint through the dark abyss to try and identify who it was. And the smell: a foul, stinking, rotting smell was carrying through the air and making the air grow thick.

"Paul?" She called out. "Is that you?"

The figure stopped for a moment, and then crouched down to all fours and started to crawl like some kind of hellish creature, rapidly picking up its pace, and snarling out with a cry that sounded part human, part something else. Haley felt a scream rising up into her throat, when she suddenly felt a hand grip her around the arm, and she yelped out as she spun around, but gasped with relief when she saw Aaron and Erica standing there, pulling her away from the approaching thing that was crawling at them.

"Run!" Aaron yanked her away just as the figure sprang up to stand tall and lash out at her, just barely missing her and collapsing into the dirt. Aaron ran so fast, and she desperately tried to keep up with him and Erica as they ran into the trees, zig-zagging around and eventually stopping as Aaron pulled her down with him, covering her mouth to stifle her loud breathing. The three of them watched as the figure, clearly a man, with his exposed skin looking blue and partly frozen, with chunks of flesh black from frostbite and decay, missing in large patches on his arms, neck and face. He had long, stringy hair and a scraggly beard caked in blood. Lifeless black eyes somehow picked up the light of the moon and seemed to glow as they darted around, searching for them.

Another camper, a young man, called out.

"What's with all the racket, Pal?" he said, annoyed. The gaunt figure, wearing a tattered fur coat and buckskin pants, spun around and roared out, causing the man to scream in terror and run back towards the light of his fire. More figures, seeming to birth from the darkness, suddenly appeared, cutting him off, and tackling him to the ground. His screams turned wet as they swarmed him, tearing his face off as they bit into him to feed, and viciously pulling at his arms and legs until they tore free from his torso with a sickening *pop!*

"What the hell are they?" Haley whispered, feeling like she was going to pass out from fear.

"Dingman's lost caravan," Erica said. "We told the story and didn't make the blood sacrifice. They're here to feed."

This was all too crazy. No way this was happening. Haley watched as the ravenous creatures that were once men and women disbanded after having their fill of the poor camper and disappeared into the darkness.

She could hear shrieking and monstrous battle cries ringing out in the darkness, and soon it seemed as if everyone in the campsite was being mauled and torn apart.

"We have to give them the offering!" Erica hissed out, and as Haley turned to meet her gaze, Aaron lunged on top of her, pinning her arms down to the ground over her head.

"What are you doing? Aaron?! Get off of me!" Haley tried to break his grip, but it was too strong, and he just looked at her with wild eyes.

"Just calm down, Haley. It'll all be over shortly. It'll just hurt for a little while, and then you'll be asleep and it won't matter anymore." He seemed different; crazed. Maniacal.

"You said it was just a small cut on the hand..."

"It's too late for that!" Erica screamed, climbing over and straddling her, seated in front of Aaron. "You have to give them all of your blood. It's the *only* way to give them what they want!"

Haley watched as Erica raised both hands over her head, a large blade in her grasp, glinting in the moonlight. She squirmed as hard as she could, bucking her hips with strength she didn't know she had, and rocked Erica forward, sending her careening into the dirt. Aaron fell to the side, and Haley kicked him in the face as hard as she could, hearing his nose crack and break, and causing him to yelp out in pain. She spun around to her belly and pushed herself up, just as Erica was climbing back to her feet, and then ducked and dodged the flailing attack coming at her.

Erica slashed the knife back and forth, desperately trying to stick it into Haley and spill her blood to stop the onslaught of demonic cannibals, hell bent on feasting on everyone at the campground. Haley fell back again, this time onto her back, and Erica came down on her, trying to slam the blade into her chest, but Haley kicked her in the gut, causing her to stagger backwards.

Getting up, Haley started to run towards the tent, hoping to find Camille and Jackson, but she stopped when she heard the cracking and splintering of tree trunks, and felt pine needles come crashing down on her. She saw the trees rock and sway, as if something was ripping them down, and a deep, raspy bellow roared out into the night air. Thunderous footsteps crashed down as a creature, fifteen feet tall, gaunt and emaciated, with parts human, animal and forest fused together in an unholy aberration. The creature stepped into the light of the moon enough for Haley to see it's hideous face: something that was part human, as if wearing the skin of a man as a mask, that hung loosely over the skull of a deer, with gigantic antlers sprouting upwards and jutting back, like the crown of a thousand evils sitting atop its head.

Erica and Aaron both stood in front of it, and Haley wanted to call out to her boyfriend, even though he'd just tried to sacrifice her, but the creature reached down and grabbed Erica, picking her up and then throwing her back onto the ground, smashing her body into an unnatural mess of bone and flesh, before bringing one of the thin legs that ended in some kind of cross between a cloven hoof and a human foot down onto her, grinding her into a puddle.

"Erica!" Aaron started toward the mess that used to be his ex-girlfriend, and the deer-thing from the woods slammed it's skeletal arm down into his screaming mouth, passing through his throat and blowing it open, reaching down into his guts and eventually tearing through his colon and out into the dirt. The creature stared at the shuddering and gagging figure before it, cocking its head, and roaring out; its yellowed fangs dripping saliva and blood. Using its other hand, the creature gripped Aaron's left side and peeled him in half, like the skin of a banana.

Haley screamed and the creature roared out into the air, before turning and grabbing the psychotic cannibals nearest it and skewering them onto its bony, antlered crown. She turned and ran into the campsite, looking for Camille, stopping as a woman ran frantically towards her with a group of decrepit and savage members of Dingman's caravan gnawing at her heels.

She could see the tent just up ahead, but it was torn open, and the lower half of Jackson was sprawled out in the dirt with a coil of thick, wet intestines springing out of it. Camille was screaming inside the tent and as Haley got closer, she could see two children, both frost-bitten and dead behind the eyes, fighting over Camille's severed leg.

She couldn't believe what was happening. This was everything of a nightmare pouring into the real world. The blood sacrifice. All of this was happening because she hadn't made a stupid sacrifice. It was just a little cut.

Snapping her head around to the fire pit, Haley ran over and grabbed one of the beer bottles the boys had been drinking, and smashed it over a rock. She took a shard of glass and held the point to the palm of her hand and then screamed out:

"Is this what you want? I'll do it! I'll give you your blood! I'll do it!"

The creature from the trees cried out into the night sky and stood tall, with the ravenous cannibals stopping in their tracks and turning to stare at her. The night suddenly seemed unnaturally still, and Haley held up her hand with the glass against her palm to show them all she was prepared to do what they required. The walking corpses stood perfectly still in front of her, and Haley felt herself start to laugh, uncontrollably. She couldn't believe it was all true. Every word of it. All she'd had to do was make a stupid cut...

A small child, skin pale and eyes shining an icy blue but void of any life behind them, stood before her. A young girl, maybe seven or eight years old. She didn't snarl or attack like the others. She looked at Haley's hand with the jagged glass bottle in her grip, and her dead eyes seemed to well with tears, though nothing came out of them. Haley lowered the bottle, and the child took a step towards here, cautiously.

Reaching out, the young girl gripped Haley's hand and took the bottle from it, tossing it aside. Haley felt a cold settling into her bones that she'd never felt before. It was as if the blood in her veins had completely frozen over. The girl touched her stomach, trying to tell her something. She then looked back at the giant antlered devil standing in the darkness, watching them.

"You don't want me to make the sacrifice, do you?" Haley asked her.

The little girl looked back at her and shook her head.

"They've been telling the story wrong, haven't they?"

She nodded.

Footsteps sounded behind her and as she turned, Haley saw the sneering, frozen face of William Dingman, lips peeled back over blood-stained teeth, cheeks black and rotten, nose completely gone. Dingman drew back a long, rusted rapier and then sliced Haley's head off of her neck, sending it bouncing to the ground, with her body crumbling to the earth next to it.

Dingman looked at the small child for a moment, and then the massive antlered creature from the woods grunted, cried out, turned and wandered back into the darkness to become one with the trees again. The night grew still and the members of Dingman's caravan finally felt a warmth in their stomachs they hadn't for a century. Their skin started to warm and turn from the lifeless blue to rosy, warm and alive.

They were at last free, and the hunger had subsided. The cursed thing from the trees that fed on them every time blood was spilled in their name was finally gone, and they could leave this in-between world they were trapped in. For years they had sat in the darkness, unable to feed, and listened to people tell their story. But it wasn't until tonight that someone took the time to face them. Someone had finally let them roam this realm. The others had all marked themselves with cuts, keeping them at bay. Their blood powering the Wendigo demon that had hunted them for ages. But this one truly feared them. They'd suddenly been allowed to leave the clutches of the forest and eat. Their curse was over.

Dingman looked up at the night sky and drew in a deep breath, feeling his stomach gurgle and groan. He looked down at Haley's corpse and smiled at the thought of that first bite.

The Sleepover III

The film faded to a wash of sepia, popped, and went black. No credits, no swell of horror-trope soundtrack. Nothing; just darkness, almost as though something within the Zenith decided it'd had enough of its mortal-electro coil.

The four boys sat, in rapt silence, pondering what they'd just watched. The room was bereft of movement and sound.

Until Brent raised his arm, pointed to the screen, and whispered, "The fuck?"

Sean stood and gingerly made his way to the television. After a single slap to the side of the beast, he looked back to his buddies and, with a mask of terror on his face, spoke the four words he feared the most.

"Dad's gonna kill me."

Dillon stood. "That's all you've got to say about the masterpiece of cannibalistic fetishism we just watched?"

Brent turned to Dillon. "Fetish? What magazines have you been reading, dill weed?"

"Guys," Sean silenced the bickering friends. "What's up with Jack?"

Jack remained seated, staring toward the TV, as though he were unable to look away.

"Dude, you're creeping me out." Brent approached Jack, but before he could get within arms length a bell chimed, frightening everyone but Jack, who fell into bouts of uproarious laughter.

"Oh, fuck, you guys are too easy. You thought I was under some satanic, cannibalistic spell. No, wait, a cannibalistic fetish spell. Hold on, let me get my gimp suit on."

Sean cocked his arm to slug Jack, but was stopped short by another ring.

"Douchemaster," Dillon flicked Sean in the ear. "It's your door."

"Probably the pizza. Be back in a bit." Sean hit the bottom stair, but stopped and looked back. "No making out while I'm gone."

Sean vanished up the stairs.

Dillon cautiously approached the VCR. A dim red glow emitted from within. He pushed the door open and the light grew far brighter than what it should. At the same time, a low thrumming sound poured from the machine—not mechanical in nature. The sound was a bleak chorus of humming in a thick, minor chord.

Brent and Jack approached the curious Dillon, with trepidation, eyes wide and curious.

"What kind of fucking VCR is that?" Brent asked.

"Sony," Dillon answered.

"Designed by Satan himself?" Jack asked with a puckish grin across his lips.

"Dudes," Sean shocked the trio from their investigation. "I told you: no making out. Besides, we got 'za!"

"Hell yeah!" Brent nearly attacked Sean. "I'm starving. Just hand me a box and I'll go over to the corner and enjoy life for about five minutes.”

Brent grabbed the top box, flopped onto the couch, opened it, and took a great sniff. “Oh fuck yeah, pepperoni is my world.”

“Dillon.” Sean handed a box over.

“Don't mind if I do.”

“And Jack, your cheese pizza—hold the meat, hold the flavor.”

Jack flipped Sean a pair of birds before grabbing his box.

Through a massive wad of dough and cheese, Brent said, “Where'd you get this pizza?”

“Pizza Shack. Why?”

“I don't know, man, pepperoni tastes strange.”

Dillon laughed. “Maybe it's human meat.”

“Not funny fucktart.” Brent tossed a grease-filled wad of napkins at Dillon.

“Let me have a taste.” Sean leaned over, snatched a round of pepperoni from the pizza, and popped it into his mouth. “Okay, I get where you're coming from. That shit's as rank as your ass. That's Brentaroni right there.”

“Kick rocks, muncho.” Brent snarled and returned to his pizza, picking off the oddly-flavored meat.

The foursome fell into silence, as they continued the feast. After fifteen minutes of nothing but chewing and swallowing, the VCR whirred back to life and kicked out the tape.

The TV flickered back on, just as Jack howled in pain.

"Oh, fuck."

"Dude, what's wrong with you? You're gonna wake up the entire neighborhood."

Jack sat his pizza box down and pulled up his shirt. "My gut's on fire, like—"

"Son of a bitch." Brent stood and pointed. "What the hell's going on with you?"

Jack glanced down at his exposed flesh to see a tear had manifested across his stomach. There was no blood, just an all-too-obvious gash that exposed the fascia beneath.

"Oh my god, oh my god, oh my god." Jack grabbed at the flesh, attempting to pinch it back together. When he squeezed, a bolt of pain raced through his system, threatening to take him down for good. "Make it stop!"

Brent knelt beside Jack and took a closer look. "What the…" He pointed. "There's a goddamn letter under there."

"Are you high, Brent?" Dillon got down on the floor to examine the wound.

"I wish I were. It'd certainly be less of a shit show than this."

With an abundance of caution, Dillon pulled away at the flesh to reveal not just a letter, but a word.

who

"Wait," Dillon blurted out with a bit too much enthusiasm. "There's more."

"Don't you fucking dare, Dillon." Jack was near panic.

Dillon pulled the flesh apart further, sending Jack into apoplectic fits of pain.

"Who am I?" Dillon spoke softly. "And it's in all lower case without a question mark."

"What the hell Dill-O? Are you the grammar police now?" Sean smacked Dillon across the back of the head.

"No, dude, just reporting my findings is all."

"Okay, Nancy Drew. But we gotta take Jack to the hospital or something. I don't want Shrimp Boat dying on us."

"Eat my shorts, Sean."

Before Sean could reply, the TV screen filled with static and a loud hiss escaped the speakers. The glow from the display seemed to highlight the third tape with an eerie glow.

"Jesus," Dillon whispered.

"What is it? The rapture?" Brent teased.

"No." Sean pointed at the tape. "Look at the title of that movie."

"Who am I?" After Dillon voiced the name of the film, all went silent and the lights went out—save for the electric snow dancing on the TV screen.

"Holy fuck."

"What is it, Jack?" There was honest concern in Sean's voice.

Jack stood, made his way to the TV, turned, and displayed the perfectly healed flesh of his stomach.

"Okay, that's fucking weird," Brent said as he returned to his pizza.

"It's a goddamn sign is what it is," Dillon added.

"For what?"

Dillon glared at Sean and then pointed to the tape. "That we watch the next film."

"Fine. If you think you can handle it."

"I can handle your mom," Dillon grinned that his standard comeback was so perfectly timed.

"Bite me," Sean answered with his own standard.

"Just sit your ass down so we can get on with the show," Brent said through a mouthful of pizza.

"You got it. Let's all answer the question, 'Who am I?'"

WHO
AM
I?
HORROR
BY JACK WALLEN

who am i

by jack wallen

kafka
he wakes thinking of kafka
broken dreams of dangerous things
thoughts disjointed like joints of broken
marionettes that swing in a childhood park
surrounded by desolation and loss
his very own metamorphoses
from man
to what

kafka

a cockroach rolling about on his bed where
his wife should be sleeping
sleep
it comes in fits and spurts these days
broken bouts of REM interrupted by abject
fear that she might awaken, reach down his
throat, pull out his heart, and swallow it
whole
his carrion crow companion

kafka

am i the roach, or is she he asks as he wakes
from a sleep born of an inner struggle he
couldn't quite place.
something was WRONG
the trajectory of his life had gone astray like
a bullet ricocheted off an anvil
w-r-o-n-g

what am i the thought rang through the bell
of his skull
i was something diff..er...ent
the word itself was shattered
a broken bell in a glass jar

or maybe the more important question was:
who am i

there it is, the heart of his darkness

who
am
i

"get up"

her voice carried with it the usual
disappointment
as if to say *oh great, i woke up next to you
again*
there was a never-ending stream of
unfettered resentment these days
eye rolls
sneers
button pushing

it all began...

doesn't everything

but where
where did this nightmare landscape start
birth
too easy

but it was all too easy
no place to land the blame

no
the splinters in his mind's eye weren't
inserted by parents or failed dreams
but
the answer existed just beyond the borders of
his memory

"get the fuck up"
again with the voice
his only recourse was to roll out of the bed of
rejection
piss
coffee
shower
shave
eat
leave
he made his way through the kitchen
grabbed an energy bar and sucked in a
lungful of optimism
his life would begin outside the house
beginnings were painful

"is that your lunch" she asks with eyes
boring holes through his heart
"watching your girlish figure I see" another
kick to the gut or a setup for a hammer that
was about to fall
"when did you care what you looked like" an
oldie but a goodie
but not the endgame

here comes the punch line to the jarring joke

"having an affair"

it was as much statement as it was question

he wasn't
he didn't have the energy for such dalliances
not these days
not with her slicing into the meat beneath his
skin to dance upon his heart
he barely had time to exist
to be something
or not to be

that question could be the answer to
everything

hamlet was always his hero

thoughts of the dane carried him back to a
better life another existence

remember what you were

the whispered voice tightened his throat with
so much regret he was not sure if his lungs
would be capable of drawing in enough
breath to continue

he did remember
everything
every moment of his life prior to the change
that swept him from everything he loved
his passion

his truth

he dropped into his car
bmw—the monument to everything he hated
about his now life
the life he never wanted
the life he'd been forced to accept
til death do you part
but death came slowly
piece by piece
bit by bit

she wanted him to be something he wasn't
first class upper middle caste
16 carat gold bullshit with cufflinks to match
only that wasn't him
not his role

what are you going to do today?

the question was a song in his ear, sung in a
cocteau twins lingering tone
the voice not his, not his usual inner
monologue

"i don't understand" he dared answer

of course you don't the response was spoken
through compressed distortion such that the
words were almost indecipherable
you only understand one thing

he smirked as though conversation with a
disembodied voice was perfectly normal

*you're tethered to a nightmare of your own
making*

a sigh

he pressed number 8 on his stereo
his favorite
all eighties all day

the fixx
secret separation

before cy curnin could sing the first word, his
phone rang
the bmw was fully equipped
he hit accept on the steering wheel

"who is she" the accusation stung
not because there was even the slightest
veracity to the question
but because she dared ask after he had spent
the better part of his adult life proving to her
his undying love and loyalty

it wasn't enough
it was never enough
nothing would or could ever be enough

she wanted so much
and more than anything in the world, she
wanted some swarthy casanova in bed
to "fuck her like she was a woman"
instead she wound up with a "passionless
limp dick"
her words cut deep
she didn't care

never did
never could
she was not wired that way
the irony being she called herself an empath
he knew the truth
empathy was a buzz word for her to share on
social media to make her look better than the
other wine sipping, han solo fashionistas for
whom truth was spoken through thumbs up
emojis that laughed and cried and cared

just another commodity
a badge of self importance
a brand in a mirror reflecting a secret reality
known only to the select few
the two comma club
decimals over decency
profit over people

she didn't even give him a chance to answer
this was never intended to be that kind of
call
it was just an opportunity to push his
buttons before he arrived at the daily grind
plant another seed of doubt in his mind
a thorn to remind him
she was always
there
watching
bitching
hating
and
being disappointed

cy finally sang

it was one of those moments where he was
certain the universe was trying to tell him
something

anything

she does not love you

the voice of the angel
or devil
who knows
returned

"then why is she with me" he decided it was
time to play along

without interaction, the station changed
pink floyd
"money"

"no" was all he said, before switching the
station back
cindy lauper "money changes everything"

"you are wrong"

silence

another station
rush
"big money"

"i said, you are wrong"

emptiness

a sigh escaped his lips, a slow motion steam
engine pulling into the station for
disembarking passengers and dumping off
the luggage of life
heavy
heavy
luggage
baggage
the weight of worlds and war on his back

he pulled into the parking lot just in time to
stop a whirlwind of emotion from consuming
his every thought and moment
before him stood the monument to capitalism
he dreaded every monday through friday
from eight to six figures
futures
stocks
money
money
money

this was not who he was
he was an artist
an actor
and once upon a time there'd been a tv show
a two camera comedy with scripts and
directors and makeup and trailers and
adoring fans
but then hollywood was fickle and bubbles
made of dreams were easily popped

he was a guitarist

and there'd been a band
they were just getting big when the singer
shot too much liquid dreamscape into his
veins and took a wild trip to the forever six
feet under
his dreams of platinum album sales tours
and worldwide fame fizzled out before it had
the chance to launch him into the outer
space of celebrity

the debt collectors came calling wolves at his
door
and in a moment of desperation he'd pulled
in a few favors to start a *career*

and then came her
the sister of the CEO
how could he say no

he could not
he did not
he should have

hindsight might be 2020
but 2020 was a really shitty year
cataclysmic

their very first date
she stared at him across an expensive meal
he could not yet afford
and mocked his choice of entrees

"you eat like you are poor"

"i am"

"no you are not" another sneer "you work for
my brother" a declarative eye roll "he doe not
hire poor people"

"guess he made a mistake with me"
I knew that was true but

she laughed
the sound was not that of angels
a chorus of wickedness sprang from deep
within her throat
actual contempt ruining what should have
been a song of joy
it was a sign
a red flag
a warning of wicked things to come

why did you not leave

the voice returned

"there was something about her"

the breasts

"no"

the legs

"shutup"

the sex

"you know i—"

he fell silent
standing in the parking lot
beside his bmw
he found himself at a loss for words for the
first time in what seemed like forever
words never escaped him

"you know i—"

he couldn't complete the thought

i do know the voice whispered *which is why i
am here with you now*
there was something soothing in the tone
and timbre of the voice
you need me

a scoff

you will see
the voice fell silent for a moment and all
thought ceased
sweet relief from the swirling chaos within
his mind

he closed the car door and began the short
walk

inside
the building smelled of disinfectant and
polish
the ceo demanded a spit shine on every
surface
worked the cleaners to the bone
paid them next to nothing
they were not worthy of his respect

for that you had to make him money
bill billions and you were a golden child
otherwise you were nothing more than a
cigarette butt to be snuffed beneath the heel
of his custom italian loafers

"waddup dawg" a clone tossed a ten
thousand dollar smile his way "take me to
the pound"

the clone offered his fist to bump
it was a ritual that made him want to break
things
hurt people
die

but this was the land of plenty and in order
to drink at that well one must blend in with
the village idiots
and so he did pound
"brocephus" the clone nodded "that's some
actionable shit right there" the clone walked
away resetting his roll

you wanted to kill him didn't you

"fuck you"

"me" another clone asked "you talkin to me"
failed attempt at a bronx accent
not funny
not entertaining
stupid clones

he stopped

"no"

dead in his tracks

"i was—"

what

"—thinking out loud about some douchebag
who cut me off on the drive here" he
swallowed the lump of lie "nearly hit the
beamer"

you deserve an oscar for that
there was honest pride in the voice
i bet it hurt to say
i bet you want to ram your face through a
window

"what i want is for you to shut up"

silence

"dude" the clone huffed and walked off

"why are you doing this to me" he demanded
of the voice

to wake you up
to bring you back from the dead

"i am not dead" he whispered

if you are not living
you are dead

at his office he shut the door
sealing out the callous world beyond
all he could think of was vanishing
leaving behind this mortal coil
composing a song to the siren that beckoned
him come play

"i told you"

it was not you who told me
it was the other you
the you that exists beyond your truth
your second skin
the skin we are going to peel away
shed your original sin

"i do not understand"

you will
in time

his phone rang
he hated the sound because it meant he had
to play the one role he loathed
a script of spreadsheets and agendas
boards of directors and whiteboards of
soulless bullshit

truth be told
he wanted to understand
but understanding took energy and effort
of that he had little to spare
he had barely enough life to move from day
to day
moment to moment

all he could think about was curling up in a
ball under a bed and sleeping away the last
remnants of his life
which was no life at all
he knew he had become a prisoner
but to what

another question that begged an answer

he picked up the phone
"in my office"
the ceo
angry
"now"

the call ended without explanation
none needed
he knew what was coming
understood it to its sickening depths
this eventuality had been building for
months
devolving from golden child to abject failure
tumbling down the charts in spectacular
fashion
his end was nigh

"your numbers have continued to plummet
month after month" the man was blood in the
face angry "give me one good reason why i
should keep you on"

he opened his mouth to speak

"and do not dare say my sister"

silence

"pack up your shit" the ceo dismissed him
with nothing more than a quick flick of the
wrist "you are done here"

about damn time the voice was soft and calm
a mother's kiss on the forehead

"go to hell"

the three words were meant for the voice
but reality was completely unaware of the
duality within his mind

"what was that" the ceo bristled "you want
any chance of a severance"
here it comes
"you damn well better kiss the ring of the
king"

don't you dare
this time the voice was fierce
it knew what was about to happen and it
would not allow another act of self-loathing

the voice grew seductive
unleash your beast

he needed little coercing
he slammed his fists down on the six figure
slab of rainforest teak
pens rattled
an autographed baseball dropped from its
perch and bounced to the floor
the ceo bristled

stood
fingers white from clenched fists
face bleeding red

"you just fucked yourself" the ceo clenched
his jaw one ratchet too tight
he would regret that tonight
his head on a down pillow
tension building to a migraine flood drowning
the synapses of his brain

he leaned across the desk
a sneer painting his face with rage
with trembling hands he reached across the
desk and grabbed a fistful of hermés silk

do it
end him
you have earned it

he yanked the tie hard
until his brother in law's face was inches
away

"say it" the ceo spat "coward"

silence

"exactly what I thought"

if you do not
i will

the voice offered a measured warning

"no" he replied

as you wish

the voice stretched its wings within his body
spread them far and wide
until it took over motor function and will
he twisted that knotted silk around his fist
for what
he didn't know

before he had a chance to stop the action
the voice insisted he yank the tie downward
and
ceo head met ceo desk

"fuck"

no golden parachute exploded from his back
to protect him from the violence at hand
no gaggle of thugs entered the room to stop
him from dropping the metaphorical hammer
over and over

"stop" he shouted at the voice

the voice did not heed

blood began to pool on the polished surface
creating
a crimson mirror reflecting the freakshow
face of a man who deserved every blow

the voice finally released his hand
the ceo dropped to his seat
and then to the floor

motionless
at least at first
seconds ticked by
minutes
eventually the ceo moaned and moved ever so
slightly

what are you doing the voice demanded *get
out*
run the fuck away

"what are you doing" the ceo snapped "did
you need something"

"i—"

he had no idea what was going on

the voice had wound tendrils of confusion
through the muck and mire of his
consciousness until there was nothing left
but a field of doubt

"go on then" the man behind the desk
dismissed him "back to the numbers"

it be would be perfectly splendid the voice
caressed his inner ear *to crack open his skull
and watch his clockworks spill out onto the
floor at his feet*

"no"

the ceo sat up straight in his chair "excuse
me"

there it is the voice tickled his instinct *your chance*

"sorry sir" he cowed "i meant my first duty of
the day was collating reports"

"well then" another dismissive gesture "have
at it"

coward

back out in the pit of the office
the khaki clones were milling about
doing worker bee things
hourly and salaried chores to help make the
company owners more money than god

buzz buzz little bees the voice laughed *you
would love to swat them down
ruin their inner workings and crack their
bones like twigs*

"wuzzap playah"

*kill him
just fucking kill him*

on a nearby desk a letter opener begged him
"come play"
he snatched up the blade
spun it in his fingers like a deft drummer
and rammed it
to the hilt
into and through the eye of one clone
eye of the dorknado

i

"who am i" he asked as the lifeless man fell
backward
his unsealed eyeball making a sick sucking
sound as it peeled away from the blade

"are you seriously going to leave me hanging
like this" the clone stood again
his eye whole
his palm hovering in the air
waiting to be slapped

do not

he slapped the proffered palm

just for that the voice grew dark *we'll have
some fun*

he casually strolled around the office
each employee he met
he ended
snapping necks
slicing arteries
piercing temples
impaling
breaking
flaying
flensing
blood spewed and arched in monochromatic
rainbows

as he continued
he wept and cried out "this is not me"
and yet it was

his secret self unleashed upon the
unsuspecting clones
no matter how hard he fought against the
voice
he had become nothing more than a puppet
a deadly pinocchio puppet
his actions not his own
and yet they were
his hands
his eyes
his maniacal laughter
echoing off the beige walls of the beige office

when the last of his colleagues dropped to
the floor he buried his head in his hands and
sobbed

"you okay duder" a familiar voice
an accountant who worked in an adjacent
office
young guy
early thirties
popped collar and sockless loafers
tesla in the drive jaguar in the garage and
a well diverse portfolio

he opened his eyes
the office wasn't strewn with dead bodies
the walls not spattered with blood and brain

wouldn't it be glorious

without another word
he marched out of the building
no one stopped him

no one cared
they all had business to attend to
money to make for those higher up the food
chain

"that's not me"

how do you know

"because i am not a violent man"

perhaps not the old you
the you before she
but the new you the you you now wear is
monstrous kept waiting hungry
wants nothing more than to end the banal
suffering of those in your orbit
poised ready to cull the herd
mow down mediocrity
make room for those deserving of a continued
existence
however few they be

your heart races at the thought
your pulse dances at the exquisite sensuality
of disrobing yourself
rending life from life after life
announcing who you are
stripping away the facade of humanity and
humility

"no" his own voice barked from his throat
"leave me alone"

a stillness pervaded and perverted the area

like a fog had settled in around him to white
out the static and hum of life
his mind flashed back to the killing field
and for a second he felt alive
connected to something other than the
drudgery
of merely existing
that thread of thought cut through the veil of
disreality to wind its way back to the before
the before time
before he found himself at the center of a
maze of confusion and schizophrenia
imaginary voices urging him to deadly
delusions
he knew he'd lived a previous life
one of ease
one of joy
of art and hope
and profound connection to the world around
him

there is a way back the voice soothed his
pounding heart *there is always a way back*

"so I can kill for you"

no the answer was sharp *so you can return to
zero
finish what had only been started
your life*

"before her"

before her

he stood

slowly
reverently
he knew where to find the answer to the only
question that mattered
was how to reclaim the one version of himself
that he ever cared for

the bmw sat
gleaming in the mid-day sun
flecks of metallic silver glittered within the
onyx paint
he once considered it the most beautiful
thing in his life
a conclusion that should have served as a
bellwether for his downward spiral
into the abyss of soulless greed
he casually withdrew his keys and clutched
one between his thumb and index finger
with as much precision as he could muster
and a dreadfully shaking hand
he scratched the question deep into the hood
of the car

who am i

with the work complete he strolled off
leaving the car behind

well done

he walked
calm
persistent
ignoring traffic
nearly run down by a truck
a car

a taxi

this life was his to lose
it had never been his at all
at least not the last decade
since that day that fateful day
he'd lived in another skin
his true self hidden behind a false face
a facade
a lie

and there was work to do
an unsung melody
a wrong to right
a battle to win
a war to end

good the voice cooed

his journey meandered through
neighborhoods
manicured lawns
two and a half car garages
two and a half children
picket fences
and 401ks
insurance
and playdates
9 to 5 zombies
stomping toward the weekend
for forty eight hours of mind numbing relief

the american dream that never was
til death do they part
and part and part again

all lies the voice spoke truth to the power of
his mind *but you see that now*

he nods now to the voice

*and what are you going to do with that
information*

"end the lie" he stopped himself "my lie"
his mind flew back to another moment
the first time they made love
she was a spirited partner
always wanting more
never really satisfied with what he could
deliver
after a while she began to refuse
saying he could never finish the job
was not capable

"i want to take a lover" she said one night
"someone who could actually please me"

he had no answer for her
a theme in his life
assumed it a joke
and moved on

one night she brought someone home
a rather large man
in every conceivable way
he caught them in their bed
she insisted the lover complete the task as he
watched
he threatened to leave
she threatened to take everything he had

eventually she promised it was out of her
system
that it would never happen again

another lie

it did

the same threats were made
lover after lover
threat and counter threat
button pushed
trap laid
game
set
match

eventually the game grew old and she tired of
pushing that particular button
so she moved onto others

his salary
his height
his fear
his weight
his voice
his friends

the accusatory glances and accusations were
never ending
so too were the rolling eyes
and mocking laughter
each fight ended with him walking out
driving a mile or two

only to return
and apologize
for what he never knew
it was not like he was perfect
he knew he had his flaws for which he spent
an inordinate amount of time atoning
it never made a difference
nothing did
no matter how he changed or evolved as a
man or a husband or a lover
it all went back to her being lonely or bored
or ashamed or over it

you are clad in the armor of splendid suffering
and that will be the undoing of those who
dare remake you in the image of their
choosing
the voice spoke a truth he had never wanted
to hear
words that were as much pain as they were
truth

a sudden buildup of pressure within the
confines of his skull
a tectonic shift in the bony plates beneath
his scalp
cracking and popping
as he stared at a billboard displaying a model
clad in bra and panties
blood red satin
a targeted ad
but for who
not he
in that moment the woman came to life
pointed at him
and laughed

shook her head
lowered a single bra strap

"you might as well put these on" the model
chided "complete the emasculation for her"
the model winked. "you might finally turn her
on"

"fuck you" he screamed until his voice
cracked

yes the voice purred *welcome your rage*

he picked up a rock
the size of a baseball
and hurled it at the woman
the projectile careened off the billboard and
crashed through a window
a store pimping secrets and desires

run the voice insisted

he refused
the thread of cowardice had been unwound
from the double helix of his dna
there was no longer a need to run
for fear had drained from his conscience
his spine metaphorically doubled in size

"no" he grinned "i will not run" he drew in a
cleansing breath "i will not hide"
he walked away from the scene of his crime
casually
as though driven by innocence and
confidence

fueled by a fattening sense of purpose

from behind
an alarm rang out
voices shouted
at him
who knew
who cared
not he
not any more

a song sprang into his head
metal health
quiet riot
frustrated
outdated
overrated

"fill the crack" he asked of the voice

*you have crawled back into the crawl space of
your mind*

"to what end"

to reclaim your truth

"kafka"

his metamorphoses was beginning
he could feel it crawling beneath his skin
some profound transformation
that would remake him from inside out
remake him in the image of what he once
was
allow him to recover what he lost

control of his own narrative
to take back control over his own narrative
from the succubus that had dared drain him
of his hunger and his heart

his journey ended
where the downward spiral began
the house he called a home
though it was no home to him
it was a cage
an institution of regression
the delilah to his sampson
the lorena to his john

nightmarish visions flashed behind the lids of
his eyes
blood
viscera
skin
bone

some premonition of a slaughterhouse
where the cattle awaited their demise
with lowing sounds
and stomping hooves
or worse
would he bathe in the blood of she who was
once his lamb
let it fall silent
that sheep
will bleat no more

the keys were still gripped tight in his fist
the house key speckled with flecks of costly
black

a scar on his upper middle class ruse
he inserted the metal tool into the lock and
gave it a quick twist

the heavy oak door whooshed open
mausoleum air
chilled by the best hvac units money could
buy
there was a florid scent
he hated that smell
roses and honeysuckle
it made his head throb and his pulse race
reminding him of a perfume
that first date
a tragic mistake

that memory would soon be washed away
by a sticky scarlet rain

"in the kitchen my dear" her voice rang out
there was a tone in the melody
unfamiliar to him
a flirtation
a seduction

she thinks

"I know" he stopped the voice short

much to his surprise
there was no build up of rage nor lessening
he was still content with his plan
to end it all
here
and

now

she whisked out of the kitchen
naked
breast implants
that he purchased
bouncing joyfully towards him

their eyes met
she covered herself

the irony

he knew every inch of her body
had reveled in its bounty countless times
touched it with wanting
but rejected
fingers

"what are you doing home" she asked with
vitriol fueling her words "you"

"live here" he answered with a robotic voice "i
pay the mortgage"

"you should be at work" she spat

"who is it this time" the question was calm
"my best friend" he answered himself "my
brother" again "my father"

she grabbed an apron from the kitchen "no
one you know" she tied the belt around her
waist "i didn't hear your car"

"i abandoned it"

"you never leave work"

"i'll never go back"

her eyes nearly shot from their orbits her jaw
practically unhinged "what" she shouted
"you" her body was shaking "no" she pointed
"no no no no no no"

"yes" he answered simply

"i have—" she fell silent

let her finish the voice interrupted *this is
delicious*

he smirked "you have what"

"a lifestyle to uphold"

the bomb dropped
detonated

tell her the voice insisted *let her in on your
little surprise*

"your desires are no longer relevant to the
situation"

"what do you mean" her voice belied her
usual haughty nature
gone was the arrogance
the audacity
replaced by fear

"i have no need for you now"

she backed into the kitchen
and returned with a knife in her grip

"stay away from me"

he laughed
from the gut
it felt good
to laugh
to finally experience the slightest bit of joy
even when said joy was at the cost of her
safety
her sanity

he took a single step toward her
the motion brought her to tears

"what are you going to do to me" she belted

there it is the voice hissed *your opening
take it*

he took yet another step forward "that" he
whispered "you always have a way of making
it about you" he reached out and grabbed the
knife from her hand "did you ever bother to
stop and think that sometimes it might be
about someone else" he spun the blade
around his nimble digits "i forgot" the blade
stopped with the deadly point inches from
her throat "you are incapable of thinking
about anyone but yourself" he chuckled

"almost poetic" he ran the edge of the blade
up her arm "how you manipulate everyone
and everything so that it perfectly aligns with
your needs and wants"

he pulled the knife away
it sang a deadly song

"that ends now"

she covered her face with her arms and
screamed

again
he laughed
as he turned away

you know what to do next

"i do"

"you do what" she shouted through a neck
tightened in the grip of fear

he pulled the bathroom door open
stepped through
locked himself in

the mirror
reflected a damaged man
eyes pleading for release from the broken life

do it the voice was sweet *your truth awaits
you*

from beyond the door

she cried out
"what are you doing"

he remained silent
let her squirm in a sweaty pool of the
unknown

it was time
time for this self to depart from the living

the tip of the knife dug into the flesh at his
forehead
there was pain
enough to catch his breath

soon the voice caressed his innermost
thoughts *the pain is a blessing from a god
you never knew existed*

he pushed the blade in until the tip touched
bone
and then he sliced
above his tired brow
down his temple
to his ear

he screamed out
but did not drop the knife
blood soaked his hand
ran down his arm
tipped and tapped on the perfect white tile
below

and yet he persisted
the blade sliced through his shoulder

down his arm
around his hand and fingers
to his armpit
and along his the left side of his torso

his knees shook
threatening to drop him to the floor

be brave the voice insisted *your new world
order is about to begin*

"not sure if i can" his voice faded along with
his strength

from the other side of the door
she pounded
small fists beating out an angry rhythm
her rage came from the wrong place
not to save him
but save her
from a life of less

"whatever it is you" she stopped herself short
"i need you"

the final lie the voice rattled his skull *she
never needed you*

he inhaled deep
droplets of blood entered his lungs
the iron tang shocked him back to his task

yes the voice hissed *kafka*

"kafka" he answered

the knife went back to work
carving away the stone of his flesh
connect the dots
alpha and omega

the pain returned
devastating and yet separate
as though someone else endured the agony
and he experienced it vicariously
from the outside looking in
outside
inside
what lies beneath the skin of so many years
of doubt
misery
and punishment

time to reveal your secret self there was joy in
the voice *to answer the question*

"who am i"

"what are you saying" she cried from beyond
"open the door so we can talk"

it is time

he grabbed a flap of skin that hung down
from his hairline
blood made it hard to handle
he found a pair of tweezers
just to get it started
when he had finally peeled away enough
flesh
he grasped it in his fist

and pulled

at no time in his life
had he ever experienced such searing pain
as though the meat beneath his flesh was
licked by the flames of hell
and yet
he peeled
and like a bloody orange
his rind came away

he battled through the crushing agony
his goal to remove the costume in one piece

once he reached his chest
the covering dropped like wet cloth
almost too easily
the pain ebbed and flowed pulsing
until he gained control of his senses
convinced himself that pain was an
imaginary construct
to prevent the human being from ever finding
truth

the rebirth

and still
she cried from far away

can you see the voice asked

"i can" he smiled in the mirror
a bloody smile
teeth too white in the contrast

in a feat of contortionist twister
he worked the flesh off the back of his skull
his neck
his backside
his buttocks
his waist

he pulled off the flesh leotard until
his skin suit
slapped the cold tiles
like a wet
rubber
sack

his burning nerves eased
grew quiet
beneath his new flesh

into the shower
pulled back the curtain
cranked the cold water until it splashed
down
to wash away the thickened blood
a flood of crimson pooled at his feet
he continued cleansing
until the water ran clear

the powerful spray trickled to a stop
he stepped out of the glass shower and onto
the floor
toweled off
wiped down the mirror
to reveal his secret self in the reflection

an unknown face

but known all the same
the answer to the most important question

"this is who i am"

his new voice matched the mind's eye
whisper that had taunted him since he woke
with "kafka" on his breath

"my metamorphosis is complete"

he bent down and picked up the skin he'd
shed
draped the arms over the shower
so the face stared out
to greet the unsuspecting
and not so innocent

a flick of the wrist unlocked the door
she sat in the hall
holding her knees to her chest
sobbing
when she looked up to him
confusion lined her face

"who are you" she asked
confusion shifting to terror

he walked past
in silence
to the bedroom
the closet
taking
something nondescript
off the rack

simple
pants and tee shirt
sneakers
and cap

he grabbed his wallet
a bottle of water
and out the front door

as he stood on the porch
a shriek ripped through the house

he smiled and walked away

"kafka"

The Sleepover IV

The boys sat in silence, eyes transfixed by the television with mouths hanging open, as the final frames of the film flickered before them. With a cathode pop the television ended the screening as it had before. The eerie red glow seeped from the VCR as it spit out the tape.

"What in the Pinhead hell did we just watch?" Brent asked nobody in particular.

"I don't know," Dillon replied, "but that blood looked so real."

Jack shook his head, "That gave me the willies. I'm glad it's over."

Sean spoke through a mouthful of partially-chewed pizza, "You guys are sissies. None of these have been *that* bad."

"You just think something isn't scary if it isn't a masked killer slashing through a group of teenagers," Brent bit back.

"Yeah, dork. You lack culture and sophistication," Dillon added.

"Oh, really?" Sean was getting defensive.

"Totally, muncho. You haven't even read a book that doesn't have pictures." Brent joined the dog pile.

"Okay, smartasses. What high-brow junk are you reading?"

"Stoker." Dillon.

"Lovecraft." Brent.

"Kafka." Jack.

"Oh *sure*. Aren't you guys *so* fancy! Just sitting around with your leather-bound tomes sipping tea with your pinkies out? Bullshit."

Brent decided it was time to play peacemaker, "Calm down, don't get your panties in a twist."

"Yeah, man, we're just giving you a hard time." Dillon eased up as well.

"I think these flicks got to you a little more than you're letting on," Jack was the psychiatrist of the group, "That whole *I'm not scared* schtick is an act."

"So what if they scared me?" The defensive tone hadn't left Sean's voice.

Brent tried to offer some consolation. "That's the entire point, man! That's why we watch these!"

"That's why we watch them together," Dillon added, "Sometimes I don't think I couldn't handle some of the stuff we watch by myself."

That was what Sean needed to calm down. He'd always been the runt of the litter and was constantly trying to make up for it with a tough-guy facade. Jack, Brent, and Dillon were his best friends, though, and they knew better. Just under the surface of the armor strutted around in Sean was a big softy.

Brent threw his arm around Sean's shoulders and tightened into a head-lock before raking his knuckles across his friend's scalp. "You don't have to play Billy Badass with us, man. We're all goopy mushy sacks of guts and feelings!"

The good-natured ribbing was interrupted by another crash from upstairs. Sean wrestled out of Brent's hold. "That fucking cat! We're never going to finish our movies!"

Dillon put his hands up defensively and stepped away from the group, "I went last time and got attacked by birds. It's your turn, man."

With a frustrated sigh, Sean marched towards the stairs."Don't start the next one without me."

Once he'd reached the top he quietly snuck down the hall, listening for any sign Satan's personal hell-kitten. He'd learned that the element of surprise was best with his mom's cat. If he knew you were after him, he delighted in turning it into a game of cat-and-pissed off teenager.

He'd made it halfway down the hall when he heard the cat hiss and screech in his bedroom. Sean rushed to the door and as he opened it the cat bolted between his legs. Before he could turn around to take chase he saw that everything on his nightstand had been knocked over. He gave up on hunting down the cat with a defeated sigh and went into his room to clean up the mess. Luckily, the alarm clock wasn't broken and his comics were in good shape. The composition notebook he used as a journal had fallen open, and the words scrawled on the page caught his eye.

DON'T WATCH

"What the hell?" he muttered to himself. The uneven all capital letters weren't his handwriting, and he'd never write in red ink. He snatched up the notebook and headed back downstairs.

Jack, Dillon, and Brent were biding their time emulating their favorite WWF wrestlers.

"Okay, very funny," Sean held the open notebook out to the other three,"Which one of you dillweeds got into my journal?"

"Huh?" Brent attention broke away just enough for Dillon to kick out of his sharpshooter and send Brent tumbling forward. Jack, balanced carefully on the back of the couch, gave up on executing his high-flying stunt and flopped down onto the cushions.

"What are you talking about?" Jack asked.

Sean thrust the open pages of the notebook towards them to emphasize the message.

"This! Who wrote this?"

Dillon chuckled, "Man, you ate too much Brentaroni. There's nothing there."

Puzzled, Sean flipped the notebook back towards himself. Sure enough, the page was clean. Thinking he may have accidentally opened to the wrong part of the book to show them he quickly leafed through the pages, but the mysterious message was nowhere to be found.

"That's so weird. I swear there was a message here when I saw it in my room." He explained to the group.

"What did it say?" Brent had picked himself up from his failed submission hold.

"Nevermind, it doesn't matter."

Brent pressed, "Aw, come on. What did it say?"

"It said *don't watch.*"

The warning excited Dillon, "Oh, then we're *definitely* watching! Get the tape!"

Sean tossed the notebook towards the base of the staircase and made his way to the stack of VHS tapes.

"Okay, then. Here it is. Our final film of the night: *Final Girl.*"

130

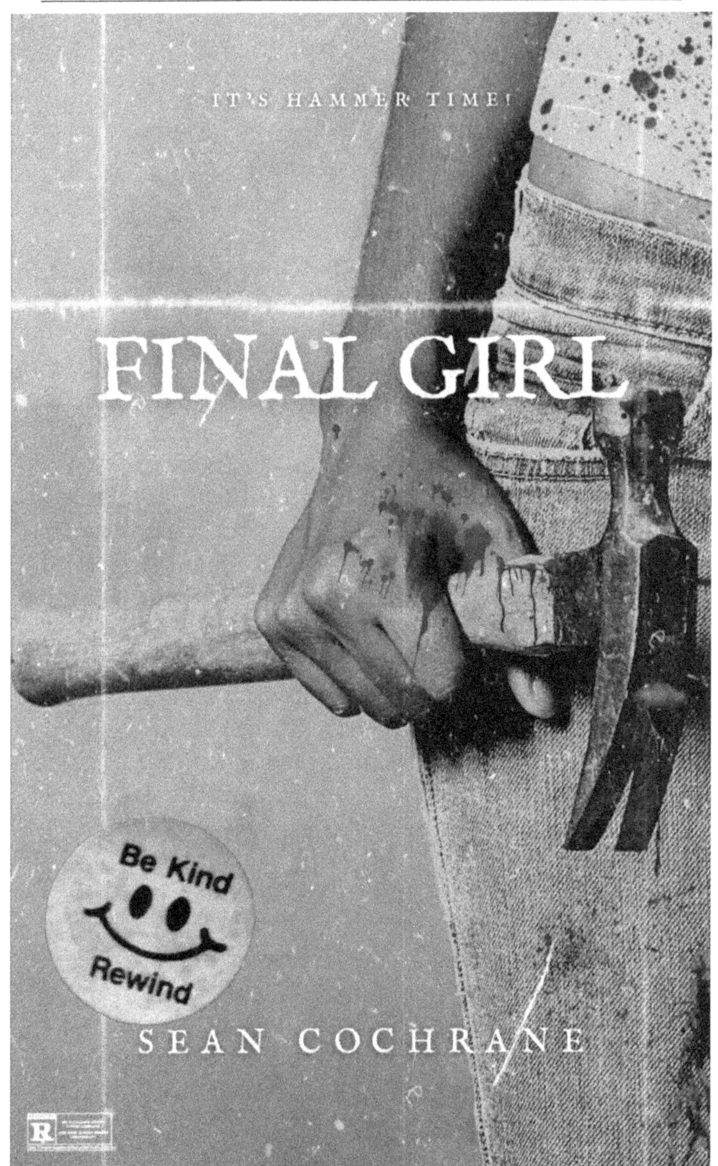
IT'S HAMMER TIME!
FINAL GIRL
Be Kind
Rewind
SEAN COCHRANE

Final Girl

By Sean Cochrane

"Stop, Jason. I'm not ready."

Jason, although begrudgingly, pulled his hand out from the waistband of his girlfriend's panties. He hadn't intended to turn into *that guy*, but he couldn't push the thought of having sex with Tammy out of his head any time they were alone together.

"I'm sorry, Tammy," the words came out as a frustrated sigh as he rolled onto his back beside her, "I don't mean to pressure you, I'm not one of those kind of guys. You know that. I just can't stop thinking about it, and I thought with my parents gone for the weekend it would be perfect."

Tammy propped herself up on one elbow, turned to face her frustrated boyfriend. "I know you're not trying to force me," her voice equal parts apologetic and empathetic, "and I trust you. I just—I don't know. I just don't feel ready yet." Her eyes shifted away from his and down to the tented front of his white briefs. "I can see you are though!" Her attempt to bring levity to the situation failed.

"It's not funny, Tammy!" It was no help to Jason that her bare chest was mere inches away. "I would never make you do something you don't want to. It's just frustrating, y'know?"

Lazily tracing a finger down Jason's torso, she made a peace offering.

"Here, I'll help you out," she affected a comically lustful tone as she pulled down the front of his underwear, "Just tell me when you're ready, I don't want you to go in my mouth again." With that, she lightly kissed his collarbone and proceeded southward.

Sunday morning arrived quicker that Jason had anticipated. His parents came home shortly after Tammy left late in the morning, giving him just enough time to hide the evidence of her stay. They immediately jumped down his throat for not completing any of the various chores they'd left for him while they were gone. Of course, he'd spent all his time with Tammy, so his entire day became dedicated to raking leaves, trimming hedges, and scrubbing toilets. He lost track of how many times he'd flipped the Slayer cassette in his Walkman—ever since *Reign In Blood* had been released the previous week he couldn't get enough of it. Jason didn't mind cramming a weekend's worth of labor into a single day. Even if Tammy hadn't been ready to go all the way he still got to spend time with her without obnoxious friends or leering parents around. By the time he'd completed his chores to his parents' satisfaction the sun was throwing its last orange and red hues into the western sky.

MONDAY

The following week started with the blur of routine. Jason spent the day doodling zombies and ghouls in his notebook as he half-listened to teachers drone on about various subjects. He wasn't worried about graduating, it was pretty much a guarantee for him. He'd entered his senior year with close to a perfect GPA, and it was no sweat for him to cram before any tests. It's not like his GPA mattered a whole lot anyway. Although he hadn't told his parents yet—his dad was going to lose his mind—Jason had no plans on going to college. Well, at least not a standard four year college. Jason's heart was set on film school. Ever since he'd seen Wes Craven's *A Nightmare On Elm Street* a couple years back his heart and mind were set on making horror movies. He hadn't really looked into it too much, but film school didn't really care about what grade you got in fifth period chemistry, did they? This year was nothing but smooth sailing for him.

When school got out at three o'clock, he met Tammy at her locker for a quick make-out session before hopping in his beat-up AMC Gremlin and heading downtown to work. Most of his friends had jobs they hated: fast food, cashier at the grocery store, gas station attendant. Jason loved his job at Cinema 2 U Home Video, though. Most nights his boss, Mr. Gallagher, had to peel him away from the television screen behind the counter of the video rental shop and force him to go home. By the time he got home, his mother would be finishing up washing the dishes from dinner. She usually fixed up a plate for him, though, and he'd just nuke it in the microwave before taking it up to his room to wolf down while taking in whichever tape he'd brought home from the horror section at work. Then it was rinse and repeat.

This Monday morning though, when Jason stopped at his locker to switch between his history and chemistry books, his routine was interrupted.

"Hey, loverboy!" Tammy popped up beside him and pecked him on the cheek. He typically didn't see her until their lunch break since their class schedules didn't coincide and their lockers were in separate areas of the school.

"Hey! Don't you have to get to P.E. right now?"

"Yeah. Coach Anderson's going to chew my ass if I'm late, but Becky just told me a few people are going out to the old Ramey Farm on Friday night. We should go."

"C'mon, Tammy," Jason protested, "You already said you'd go to the drive in with me Friday night. The new *Summer Camp of Blood* is opening. Part five. I've been waiting for this all year!"

"Oh, I can't wait!" Her eye roll punctuated the dripping sarcasm. "Let me guess, another clueless group of teenagers goes out to the woods to get drunk and fuck when the killer who died at the end of part four comes back to pick them off one by one?"

"Probably, but they brought back the original writer and director—"

"Did they bring back the same group of idiots? The jock, the nerd, the slut, the burnout, and my personal favorite: the virgin?"

"Oh, c'mon. It's not that bad. Plus the practical effects in this franchise are—" she cut him off again before he could wax philosophical on the intricacies of on-screen murder.

"Think about it. Instead of watching a bunch of teenagers get drunk and have sex in a creepy old building, wouldn't you rather *live it*? We can be the stupid kids!"

"I guess I'm the nerd and you're the virgin then, right?"

"Is that a yes?"

"Maybe. I'll check Saturday's show times. You still owe me a movie date."

"Maybe if you come to the party you'll be the nerd and I *won't* be the virgin by the end of the night..."

"Really?" Jason couldn't hide his obvious excitement.

Before Tammy could reply the hallway filled with the deafening ring of the school bell.

"Oh shit," she said as she turned to sprint towards the gym, "Anderson's going to kill me."

Jason watched the back of her Jordache jeans hungrily as Tammy jogged away. If anyone was worth missing the premier of *Summer Camp of Blood Part V* it was Tammy.

They'd been dating since just after Tammy moved to town sophomore year, and he did truly love her. Although his buddies were constantly ribbing him about never getting past third base with her—even well into their senior year—that had never been his priority. Lately, though, his more base desires had become hard to ignore. The prospect of finally crossing home plate was enough to put horror on the back-burner.

That afternoon went as usual. Jason rewound the tapes people had failed to be kind about and charged a fee to their account before restocking the days' returns. After that he sat behind the counter watching *Night of the Living Dead* for the millionth time while breaking away only to suggest movies to undecided customers, rent out movies, and answer the few phone calls the store received. Mr. Gallagher had left for a short while, as he did every afternoon, to head across the street to K-Mart and buy a TV dinner. Mr. Gallagher closed the store every night and ate his microwaved dinner when business slowed down. Jason didn't think the man had had a home-cooked dinner in years.

Jason was in the middle of restocking returned tapes when the phone rang up front. He dropped the copies of *The Breakfast Club* in his hand back onto the push cart and jogged towards the front of the store.

"Cinema 2 U, this is Jason. How can I help you?"

Silence hung dramatically on the line.

"Hello, can you hear me? This is Cinema 2 U."

Jason heard what he thought was someone breathing on the other end.

"Hey, I can barely hear you. Can you speak up?"

The breathing continued, but the caller remained speechless.

"Okay, then. We're open until ten if you need to call back."

The front door chimed as Jason put the receiver in its cradle. Mr. Gallagher carried in his Swanson's meal and a can of Diet Coke. He didn't look pleased.

"I saw Louise Meyer while I was paying for my dinner, Jason. And she told me you suggested a movie to her Friday night."

Jason cringed slightly. He knew what was coming.

"She said she'd asked you for a romance movie and you told her to rent *Dracula*."

"I can explain, Mr. Gallagher. I'd just seen Mrs. Jones' kid sneak into the adult room," he lied, "I focused on getting him out of there when Ms. Meyer asked me about a romance movie. I'm not good with romance, so I just said the most romantic story I could think of."

Mr. Gallagher eyed him suspiciously. Although he'd personally had to drag Bobby Jones out of the XXX room at the back of the store on more than one occasion, he wasn't sure Jason was being completely honest with him.

"You consider *Dracula* to be romantic?"

"Well, maybe not the movie, I guess. But in the book he gives up Heaven to spend eternity with his wife in hell. That's pretty romantic. Don't you think?"

Mr. Gallagher gave a defeated sigh. Jason was a good kid, and he didn't ever do anything *really* bad. Every now and then he'd do something mischievous along the lines of recommending a horror movie to an old widower interested in a romance film, but it wasn't worth it to push the issue.

"Just try to be more mindful with your recommendations from here on out, would you? And credit Ms. Meyer's account with a free rental."

"Right away, sir."

"Oh, who was on the phone?"

"Just dead air."

TUESDAY

Jason's mom woke him up the same way she did every morning. After cracking his bedroom door and taking an apprehensive peek inside to make sure he was properly covered and there were no hormone-induced *situations* that could prove embarrassing for the both of them, she pushed the door open fully. The aroma of teenage boy—body odor accented by old fast food and a hint of designer impostor cologne—crept up her nostrils and danced along the back of her throat. She surveyed the smoke-settled battlefield of his room. Fallen soldiers of denim, poly-cotton, and leather lay dead and dying. Gruesome faces, some living and some dead, looked down with approval from the horror movie and heavy metal posters decorating the walls.

"Jason, you've got to clean up in here. It's a pig sty. And what is that *smell*?" she pleaded, mostly to herself and only partially to her still sleeping son. She knew her words would fall on deaf ears or sleeping ears, and the latter didn't end with eye-rolling and back-talk.

After her ritual complaint about the mess, she crossed the minefield of clothing and empty BigMac wrappers to bring Jason back from the dreamworld.

"It's time to get up, it's time to get up, it's time to get up in the morning!" Jason's mom had been singing the same reveille to wake him since he was a small child. It used to be a fun, goofy pairing to the tickles she'd administer. Now it only served to annoy him to consciousness, but it was one of the last pieces of his childhood she had left to cling to. He was going to be grumpy getting up anyway; she might as well get some fun out of it, right?

"Geez, mom. Are you *ever* going to give that up?"

"Not on your life. You may be Mister Tough Heavy Metal Dude to your friends, but in this house you're still my sweet little boy." She drew the curtains on his window to let the sun in as she teased him, and Jason responded by covering his head with his pillow.

"Does the tickle monster need to make an appearance?"

"Okay! I'm up! I'm up!" Jason squinted in the morning light. "Did you have to open the curtains?"

"Yes. And luckily for you it's a nice morning. I'm opening the window, too. The stench of death and old food needs to air out of your dungeon."

Jason had already stopped paying attention by the time his mother opened the window to let the crisp autumn air in. There were only two places in his room where any sort of order or organization could be found, and those were the two bookshelves that housed his VHS and music collections. He may have been less than concerned with where clothes, trash, and other various objects landed; but his movies and cassette tapes were meticulously organized. His finger glided from top to bottom across alphabetical stacks of cassette cases, finally stopping towards the end of the "O" section. Ozzy's *Diary of a Madman* would suit the morning well.

"Shut that window before you come downstairs," his mom ordered before shutting his door. She didn't wait for a response. He had gone off to Heavy Metal Land, and she made a mental note to come back and check the window after he'd left for school.

Jason dramatically kicked around his room and shredded his air guitar alongside Randy Rhoads as he dressed himself. At the end of "Flying High Again" he'd made himself as presentable as possible—dirty denim jeans, a *British Steel* t-shirt, and tattered Converse sneakers. Jason handed the invisible instrument to his imaginary roadie, waved to a few fans, and exited the stage to go brush his teeth.

Brushing his teeth and applying some deodorant didn't take long, and he was back in his room in time to match Randy's solo in "You Can't Kill Rock And Roll".

Except Randy wasn't playing. Ozzy wasn't singing. His room was silent.

"No! No! No-no-no-no!" Jason rushed to his stereo, afraid the tape had been eaten. Oddly, the playback had stopped completely. The gears weren't continuing to turn, devouring the analog musical bliss. He ejected the cassette just to make sure it was okay, and to his relief the tape was fine. He popped it back in and pressed the play button.

Nothing.

He switched the power off and back on, then pressed play again.

Still nothing.

"Shit. You can't break. I can't afford a new stereo! It took me forever to save up for you!"

Jason frantically searched around the outside of the music box for signs of damage or tampering. As he checked the back of the stereo, he noticed the power cord had been unplugged from the outlet.

"What the hell?"

Jason knew that sometimes he could be a bit loud and carried away with his music, but the only time it was ever an issue was if his dad was working the overnight shift. His dad was a cop, and he hated working overnights. Their small town was relatively crime free, so night patrols were particularly boring and lonely. At least during the day he could stop in for friendly chats with people around town. But his dad hadn't worked the night shift for months. He'd been on the morning shift, which meant he was out of the house by a quarter to six. Jason leaned out of his room into the hall.

"Hey mom?" He yelled.

"Yes, honey!" She rang back.

"Did you unplug my stereo?"

"As much as you know I hate that racket, I haven't been back upstairs."

Perplexed, Jason turned back to his room to take another shot at playing Sherlock Holmes. In his panic over the possibility of his *Diary* tape being destroyed, he'd missed a glaring detail in the case.

The chaotic mass of dirty clothes and trash in his room had been rearranged into a message:

DONT
GO

"What the fuck is going on?"

His eyes searched around the room fruitlessly for an answer to his question. Jason stepped to the middle of his room and kicked at the message, returning the room to its previous state, before leaving to head downstairs. Just as every other morning, his mother was in the kitchen with two Pop-Tarts ready for him to scarf down on his drive to school.

"Hey, did you mess with the clothes in my room?"

"Jason, there was a time when I'd spend my days cleaning up your messes and washing your clothes. Now isn't that time. If you want a clear floor and clean clothes, you're going to have to be a big boy and do it yourself."

"Thanks mom," Jason hid his deepening confusion and pecked his mom on the cheek, "gotta go!"

"Make sure you're extra quiet when you come home tonight. Your dad got called in early to work a double."

"Oh, really?"

"Yeah, he had to dive to the prison up north to help beat back the press."

Jason stopped before he was completely out the door. His dad had been a cop Jason's entire life and working doubles wasn't anything new, but small town police being called to help with press at the state penitentiary an hour north of town was odd.

"Why? Can't the guards deal with a few reporters?"

"Normally, yeah. But yesterday someone burned the place down. Chained up every single door to one cell block. Everyone inside—guards *and* prisoners—everyone died." Her normally cheerful face had melted into a pensive frown.

"How does that happen?" Jason's mouth hung open in shock.

"I don't know, honey. I'm just praying for those dead guards." She stared glassy-eyed towards the floor for a moment before snapping to. Her morning smile and cheer returned. "But you don't need to worry about that. You just need to make sure your dad can sleep when he gets home."

"Sure thing, mom," Jason replied, "Love you!"

"Love you too, honey!"

WEDNESDAY

Something was wrong. Tammy had completely avoided Jason at school yesterday, and she hadn't answered or returned any of his calls. He'd left for school early this morning in order to be exactly where he was at: waiting at her locker. She *had* to stop here before heading to her first period English class. If she showed up without her books Mr. Barker would skin her alive. While he waited, Jason cycled through his mind a replay of the last two days for the millionth time. The odd phone call was forgotten, and the strange message was nothing more than a faint echo of a thought—all his attention was focused on figuring out why Tammy was so mad at him.

Just as he came up with nothing *again* Tammy rounded the corner from the main hallway. She stopped as soon as she saw Jason waiting, but she didn't turn and walk away. After a brief moment to steel her nerves, she crossed the distance between them. Jason didn't reach out to hug her or lean in for the typical good morning kiss. He opened his mouth to speak, but she cut him off.

"I'm not mad at you. I'm sorry I avoided you."

Jason hadn't realized he'd been holding his breath in until it rushed out of him in a relieved sigh. His worry and anger dissipated, but he was still confused as to what made her avoid him.

"Jesus, thank you. I thought I'd done something." Jason wrapped his arms around her shoulders.

"No, it isn't you." She was still on edge, her body stiff and apprehensive.

Jason withdrew from the embrace and searched her eyes.

"What's going on Tammy?"

"You know the prison up north? Some sicko locked everyone inside one of the buildings and set it on fire. Like, so people died."

"Yeah, my dad had to go and help keep the press out. It's really bad. I don't get that has to do with—"

She interjected again. "It just really messed with my head for some reason. I needed some space. That's all."

"Are you okay now?"

Tammy forced a smile and glanced both ways down the slowly filling hallway. She leaned into Jason's ear and rested one hand on the crotch of his jeans.

"Meet me at your car at lunch and I'll make it up to you," she whispered. She punctuated the lusty invitation with a quick squeeze, and instead of waiting for a response she pecked his cheek and pushed him to the side.

"Now get out of my way, I've got to get my books. If I'm late again this week Mr. Barker will make me suffer through detention, and if I get detention then Friday is off."

Friday! He'd forgotten all about the party and the promise that it would be the single most important night of his young life. An image of the message in clothes flashed behind his eyes. *Not a chance* he thought to himself, *Friday night is the night!*

Tammy finished loading her English books into her backpack and kissed him deeply before heading to class.

"See you at lunch, Loverboy!"

Jason didn't have time to make it to his own locker before History class without being late, so he'd have to deal with the consequences. More concerning to him at the moment, though, was concealing the erection she'd given him.

Focusing on class was a lost cause. Just as his mind was consumed with Tammy's distancing for the past twenty-four hours, it was now a dreamscape of lunchtime voyeuristic pornography. By the time the bell rang signaling the beginning of the lunch period his bloodstream was heavily diluted with testosterone and endorphins. He made it as quickly to his car and waited for Tammy. She arrived within a couple minutes. As soon as she'd closed the door she began unbuttoning her blouse.

"Drive to the back lot behind the football field. Nobody's ever there," she directed while twisting an arm behind her to unclasp her bra.

Jason didn't wait for further direction. He shifted his rust bucket of an AMC Gremlin into gear and got moving. As soon as they'd pulled out of view of their peers, Tammy moved his hand from the gear shift to the bare skin under her open shirt. For a brief second he considered pulling it away to shift into third gear, but he thought better and took his time driving to the deserted back lot. It wasn't until he'd come to a stop that he took his hand away to shift into neutral.

No sooner had than he'd released the clutch, Tammy was opening the fly of his jeans. Seconds later, his head rolled back in bliss as hers went down to provide it. Like something out of an advice column in a smut magazine, he closed his eyes and tried to think of anything other than Tammy's ministrations. Lemmy's moles, Kerry King, baseball—he didn't even *like* baseball— anything to draw out the experience. After an entire half of the school day fantasizing about this very moment, though, his efforts seemed in vain.

A loud thump on the roof of the car jolted him from his erotic trance, and Tammy straightened up in the passenger seat.

"What was that?" she yelped while scrambling to cover herself from any onlookers.

Jason took a quick survey of their surroundings.

"I don't know. I don't see anyone anywhere."

He cranked the window down halfway and shouted to the empty parking lot, "Hey! Who's there?" Only the sound of lunchtime traffic in the distance replied.

The abrupt stop to the sexual activities paired with the increasing feeling of panic growing in his gut softened Jason's arousal. He clumsily tucked his member back into his jeans then cautiously stepped out of the vehicle and took a few tentative steps towards the center of the lot. Again, he surveyed the area to find nothing other than some crows fighting over a scrap of trash. He turned back to the car to reassure Tammy, and the panic brewing in the pit of his stomach exploded to his extremities.

"What is it, Jason?" Tammy, now fully reclothed, asked. "Jason?"

He didn't respond to her, only stared over the top of the Gremlin—his face emotionless save the fear and disgust burning in his eyes. Tammy peered out the passenger window but found nothing alarming. She opened the door and stepped out, and when she turned to ask Jason what was wrong she screamed.

Sitting atop the Gremlin was the source of the sound that had disrupted their lunchtime rendezvous, a tin bucket filled to overflowing with viscera.

On the side, in paint faded from decades of use, but more from inactivity, the Ramey Farms Dairy logo peered out between rivulets of blood. The slenderer hoof at the end of a partially decomposed leg jutting up in the middle implied that it was only animal entrails, but that didn't comfort the teens or relieve the nausea snaking its way up their throats.

Tammy's shrill scream shook Jason from his horrified stupor.

"Get back in the car. I'm taking you home."

She scrambled back into the vehicle without question. Jason walked to the drivers side door and surgically lifted the bucket's handle, being careful not to touch any of the filth within. After gingerly placing the container of blood and entrails on the ground, he sat back in the car and drove away as fast as the four-speed engine could manage.

THURSDAY

Jason's mom didn't bother trying to wake him. She didn't apprehensively open his door praying that today wasn't the day her teenage son would be uncovered in all his glory. There was no griping about cleanliness. No playful morning cadence. No heavy metal. No air guitar.

Routine and normalcy were festering in an antique dairy farm bucket in the parking lot of the high school football field. Not even the crows were interested.

She left Jason to sleep and called the school to let them know he was sick. She knew it wasn't true, but her maternal instinct insisted that something was awry. This wasn't the typical teenager faked stomach ache. Jason drove home early from school, skipped work, and barely ate dinner. It was calling into work that tipped her off. She knew his blasé claim of illness was a lie, but he loved his time at Cinema 2 U as much as he loved to take long showers. If something was keeping him from that, it was serious. So she made the call to the school and let him sleep.

The drive to Tammy's house the previous day had been silent. Neither of them could find words to properly articulate their churning thoughts. After pulling up in front of her home, Jason only said, "Make sure you lock all the doors. I'll call you later." She nodded and exited the Gremlin. No hugs. No kisses. No professions of love. A tapestry of confusion and dread weighed on both of them. Jason's mind consumed itself with who might be harassing him on the drive home. Unable to draw his mind away from the message in clothes and the revolting bucket, he decided to fake sickness. Aside from uttering that lie to his mother, the only other words he spoke for the rest of the night were, "Hey, it's me. I can't get it out of my head. I'm staying home sick tomorrow. You too. I'll come over as soon as I can. I love you," when Tammy answered his call. He didn't wait for a response before resting the phone back in its cradle.

The long sleep was needed and welcomed, but the foreboding messages refused to vacate their place in his consciousness once he awoke. Turning to his clock radio, he noted it was just past ten in the morning.

The message was clear: someone didn't want him, or them, to go to the party out at the Ramey Farm. What wasn't clear was who or why. Jason hadn't told Tammy about the clothes yet. After her day spent avoiding him and the bucket incident he'd decided against it. Now, after some rest and time to consider things, he decided that it was necessary. It would upset her further, sure, but she deserved to know. Plus, the horror fan sitting just behind his eyes mused, it might save their lives.

It was Thursday, and that meant his mom was out of the house grocery shopping and running errands until a bit after noon. That gave him just enough time to drive to Tammy's house, tell her about the clothes, cancel Friday's plans, and get home without being caught. It took just a few minutes to get dressed and he was out the door.

Tammy lived in a new subdivision on the other side of town. It took a bit longer to get there because Jason had to avoid the main roads so that nobody—particularly his mom or dad—would see him out and about while he was supposed to be home sick. He kept to side streets and parked in front of Tammy's house twenty minutes later. Tammy was waiting for him on the front porch, sitting with her denim-covered knees pulled up to the chest of her oversized sweater. Her hair was pulled back into a messy ponytail, and as he approached Jason could tell that she hadn't gotten any sleep.

"Hey, how are you holding up?" he asked, knowing full well that any answer other than "I'm not" would be an outright lie.

"Still freaked out." Tammy honestly replied.

"You don't look like you got any sleep."

"I tried, but every time I closed my eyes I saw that awful bucket. I just laid there with my eyes open all night."

"I thought I was the one that was supposed to keep you up all night."

Jason's attempt at levity fell face first into silence.

"Yeah. Sorry. Not the time for jokes," Jason apologized, "I'm just freaked out too, and... I don't know..." his voice trailed off at the lack of excuse.

"Did you sleep?"

"Yeah, but as soon as I woke up that fucking bucket was right back on my mind. I can't shake it. And there's something else."

"Something else?"

"Yeah, I think it's connected somehow. Let's go inside though. I feel like someone's watching us out here."

"Me too." Tammy said solemnly as her eyes cautiously scanned the neighborhood.

"You feel like someone's watching?"

"And I have something else to tell you."

Before the confusion could fully wash across Jason's face, she turned to enter the house. He followed her, and this time his eyes weren't lustily fixated on her Jordaches. Instead, he focused on the back of her head and tried to solve the puzzle she'd just created for him. Tammy continued through the house and to the kitchen. She poured coffee for them both and brought the cups to the small breakfast table.

The brew had been sitting for a while; it was burnt and overly bitter, which Jason thought was somewhat fitting for the story he related in between sips. As he expected, learning of the cryptic message pulled Tammy deeper into the pit of fear and despair she was already trapped in. It wasn't just the bucket of offal and the clothes though. Something else had its claws in her, but Jason couldn't put his fingers on what it was.

"Why didn't you tell me?" she inquired plaintively.

I was going to, really, I was. But then you avoided me that whole day and I was so wrapped up in trying to figure out what was wrong that I forgot. Then by the time I remembered you'd got me thinking about lunchtime and, well, you know… I didn't want to fuck that up."

An exasperated sigh punctuated Tammy's eye roll.

"Some things are more important than blowjobs, Jason."

"I know. I'm sorry." Jason's head dropped in shame.

"Well, I didn't tell you everything either. Actually, I didn't tell you anything."

Jason looked up to see tears welling in Tammy's eyes.

"Whatever it is, Tammy, I love you."

"You love the me you know," she stood from the table and turned to both avoid eye contact and hide the first tears that quietly rolled down her cheek, "You don't know my past though."

Tammy busied herself with making a fresh pot of coffee while she continued to talk.

"I moved here sophomore year and didn't tell anyone much about where or *why* my family moved. Hell. My family isn't even really *my* family."

Jason sat in stunned silence.

"Mom and dad, the Englands, adopted me and moved here so I could start fresh. Nobody knew me. I wouldn't have to deal with the stares. I wouldn't see constant reminders."

"Of what?" Jason's question was barely whispered.

"The night before Halloween freshman year, I woke up to my mom, my *real* mom, screaming. I went down the hall to see what was wrong, and she was in the doorway of her room arguing with my dad." Tammy took a deep breath and attempted to steady her already cracking voice. "Just as I was about to say something, he swung the hammer."

"Oh shit, Tammy. I'm so sorry. You don't have to—"

"Yeah, I do. You have to know. It involves you now." Her eyes met his for a brief moment, then quickly jumped to focus on her coffee as the first tears fell. "The hammer claw caught her right in the cheekbone. The force spun her around and basically tore half of her face off. I still remember the wet cracking noise it made. Her eyes met mine and the last word she spoke was 'run'. So I ran. I didn't even know where I was going. I just ran until I couldn't anymore. I don't even remember past that point."

Tammy wiped the tears from her eyes with the sleeve of the sweatshirt and sipped her coffee.

"Someone found me the next morning. Apparently I'd hidden in some bushes outside their porch and fallen asleep from exhaustion—or shock. They called the cops, and when they found my dad he was still at home still hammering away at what was left of my mom's body. Some sleazebag lawyer got him out of the death penalty, but he got sentenced to life. I got adopted by the Englands. And here I am." She forced a weak smile, visibly attempting to fight back a second wave of tears.

Jason sat in stunned silence for a moment before responding.

"And that prison where they sent him. That's the one where the fire was?"

"Yeah."

"And you think he did it?"

"I know he did. I feel it. Like, I can't explain it, but I *know* it was him."

"And he's coming—"

"—after me to finish what he started."

This time, there was no choking back the tears. Jason moved to the other end of the table and brought his sobbing girlfriend to her feet. Wrapping her in a protective embrace, he asked one last question.

"So why the creepy messages?"

"To scare you away and get me alone."

Jason squeezed her a bit tighter before stepping back. He kept his hands on her shoulders and stooped slightly to look into her eyes.

"It didn't work. I've studied every crazed killer and every twisted mind. He doesn't scare me, and I'm not letting you get hurt. We're going to that party."

His nascent bravado surprised her.

"What?"

"Look. He's coming after you, and there's no way we can stop that. Even if he gets caught and locked up again he's going to come back, right?"

"Yeah." Her eyes searched his, trying to figure out where he was headed.

"All those times I've said I love you I meant it. I won't let him hurt you. Not now. Not ever. I'll put an end to this... or I'll die trying."

FRIDAY

Jason's mother had been surprised to find him already awake when she peeked into his room to see if he was feeling well enough to go to school. Not only was he awake, he was fully dressed, tethered to his stereo by headphones, and performing what she could only describe as an interpretive dance about an exorcism. His back was to her, so she watched his bizarre teenage ritual with intrigue.

"There's only one way out of here... piece by piece!" He hissed and stopped his violent convulsions.

"You seem to be feeling better."

Jason spun to face her, shocked and mildly embarrassed at her presence.

"Oh, uh, yeah," he searched for an excuse, "must have been a twenty-four hour bug."

"Yeah, okay. Make sure to call Mr. Gallagher and let him know you'll be in tonight."

"Oh, I've already got the night off. The new *Summer Camp of Blood* is opening tonight. I'm taking Tammy."

"I see. Well, you'd better be a gentleman and keep your hands to yourself."

"Sure thing, mom." He grinned sheepishly.

The rest of the day was uncomfortably normal. It seemed counterfeit to Jason. He and Tammy shared their typical between class pleasantries and kisses, but made no mention of the night's endeavor. The day was pretending to be normal, but an uncertain static buzzed underneath the facade.

When the final bell rang, Jason and Tammy met at his car.

"So, we've got a few hours, what's the plan?"

"Honestly, I don't know."

"What!?" The faith she'd put in him shook.

"I mean, I don't know *exactly*. These killers, they all have their own way of doing things. But, if it's a party at an abandoned farm, I'm guessing he's going to start picking off people one by one. Cause some chaos thinking he'll be able to catch you off-guard."

"And?"

"We'll be—*I'll be*—expecting him." Jason opened the trunk of the Gremlin to show her his supplies: a large fixed-blade hunting knife he'd stolen from his dad's gun safe, a baseball bat he'd driven some nails through, and a couple rolls of duct tape.

"Why the duct tape?" Tammy asked.

"I don't know. It just seems like the kind of thing you want handy in a situation like this."

With that, he closed the hatch and the young battle-ready couple got in the car and went for a bite to eat. They went about their afternoon as they would any other Friday, again half-successfully pretending it was a normal day. At eighteen years old their only way to cope with such a grave predicament was to ignore it completely until it was impossible to do so. It became impossible when dusk settled.

"It's time. Are you ready?"

"Yeah, I think so." The hesitation in her reply betrayed her, but Jason knew there wasn't another option. He ejected the cassette from the radio, flipped it, and headed toward the outskirts of town as Tom Araya screamed over the opening riff of "Angel Of Death".

The party was already going when they arrived. Jason parked the Gremlin just off the dirt drive that led up to the abandoned farmhouse. Although he wasn't sure how many people had been invited to the party, he didn't want to park on the neglected front lawn with the others and risk being blocked in by any late arrivals. Before he and Tammy trekked the remaining fifty yards to the dilapidated two-story, he emptied the textbooks and folders from his backpack and replaced them with the knife and tape. He slung the pack over his shoulder and grabbed the spiked bat. Tammy shut the hatch, and they marched forward.

The old farm sprawled around them. Aside from knee-high weeds, there was nothing other than the old home and barn left on the property. The Ramey dairy had gone out of business some 20 years prior. Samuel, the elder Ramey and fourth owner of the family business, had grown too old to continue the operation and his son was more interested in the allure of LSD and psychedelic rock than taking over the family business. A larger corporate dairy bought the farm for next to nothing, took the equipment and cattle, and left Samuel and his wife to rot. And that's what they did. After buying a small cottage home in town they two died from old age and regret. It only took a few years for the old property to become the destination for high school parties.

Jason propped the bat behind a dead bush to the side of the creaky porch steps. He kept the backpack with him, and he opened the door of the ranch house for Tammy. They were immediately assaulted by Bananarama blaring obnoxiously from a boombox. A few people turned to welcome them to the party. Notably, Linnea Quinley and Deena Prince scoffed when they saw Tammy. Linnea was the head cheerleader and sat atop the school's social hierarchy, Deena was a bookish girl she'd taken under her wing. Their friendship was solely transactional. Deena did Linnea's schoolwork and kept her grades up in exchange for social status. They both carried a particular disdain for Tammy ever since their boyfriends, star quarterback Wes and his lackey Tad, had been caught on multiple occasions ogling Tammy ass. If Linnea and Deena were around, that meant that Wes and Tad were somewhere near. The source of the thick pot smoke hanging in the air was Andrew, the school's requisite stoner. He tended to drift between social groups, enemy to none and a friend of anyone who needed a joint. Not willing to allow the insipid pop music spewing from the cheerleaders' boom box sully his high, Andrew was leaned against a wall in the unfurnished living room bopping his head to whatever was pumping through his headphones.

"So, what do we do?" Tammy asked Jason.

"Just hang out, I guess. Stay close, and don't let your guard down."

The blow came out of nowhere. A single back-handed strike to Jason's crotch. He doubled over and fought back the tears.

"Cup check Jason!" Tad howled, "What kind of nerd brings his backpack to a party?"

"Unless you've got more booze or something in there. Do you?" Wes followed up and wrestled the bag from his back before Jason could secure it. While Tad kept Jason away Wes looked at the bag's contents.

"Holy fuck Jason," he turned to Tammy and grinned wildly, "Oh, you're into some weird shit!" He forcefully pushed the bag back into Jason's arms. "Here you go, horndog!"

Noticing their girlfriends were getting pissed at the attention they'd paid Tammy, the star quarterback and linebacker headed over to make amends.

Andrew continued on, eyes closed, journeying through his own world; only aware of his music and his joint.

"Where is everyone?" Tad questioned loudly, "This party is boresville! C'mon Linnea, I have something I want to show you upstairs." After a knowing giggle with her friend, Linnea followed him up the staircase.

Without a team captain to play second place to, Wes felt the need to posture himself as the group's alpha male. Leaving Deena to herself, he sauntered over to the spaced-out stoner and flicked him in the forehead.

"You gonna share that joint or what?"

"Take it, man," Andrew offered the remainder to him, "I'm going to the barn to meet god." As he shuffled towards the door at the back of the house, the rhythmic thumping from an upstairs bedroom shook bits of plaster and dust loose from the antiquated ceiling. Linnea's unenthused moans of dramatized pleasure made the remaining partygoers cringe.

"I'm not going to sit here and listen to this." Wes took the stub of a joint and walked out to the porch.

"Aren't you going with him?" Tammy asked Deena.

"No. He falls asleep when he's stoned. You just watch. He's going to sit on the stairs, take a few puffs, and he'll be out like a light."

"So what are you going to do?"

"Drink beer, listen to tunes, and not have to put on the Broadway performance Linny's doing," she replied as she adjusted her eyeglasses on the bridge of her nose.

"You call that music?" Jason scoffed.

Before Deena could spit back a reply, Linnea screamed from upstairs. The group paused for a moment, looking at one another uncomfortably. She stopped the tape playing in the boom box.

"That didn't sound like an orga—" A second, more horrific scream interjected and was followed by a loud thump that caused more dust and chips of plaster to rain down on the three teens.

The group rushed upstairs and burst through the first bedroom door they came to. Tammy and Deena shrieked at what they saw. Despite the amount of celluloid gore he'd consumed over the years, Jason had to fight back the swell of vomit in his throat. Tad's nude body was splayed on the floor, an unrecognizable mass of blood, bone, and hair where his head once was. Linnea stood against the wall across the room. Frozen in fear, she didn't speak or even attempt to cover her naked body. The moonlight coming through the window highlighted the tears trickling from her wide eyes and the spatter of blood across her ample chest.

"What happened?" Tammy asked, although she knew the answer. The scene wasn't foreign to her.

Linnea remained silent.

"She's in shock. She can't answer," Deena said as she crossed the room to her motionless friend. "Linny!" She yelled and shook the nude girl's shoulders.

Linnea slumped forward. A sticky tearing sound cut through the quiet room as the combination of dead weight and the force of Deena's shake dislodged Linnea's corpse from the hay hook hastily nailed to the wall.

Deena screeched and stepped away from the body and began to cry when her eyes met the chunk of flesh and spine remaining on the hook.

"We've got to go tell the others," Jason commanded.

The trio descended the stairs and headed for the porch to warn Wes. At the top of the porch stairs where they'd expected him to be nodded off in a purple haze, they found a hatched resting in a pool of blood. Wisps of steam rose from the puddle into the chilled night air.

"We have to leave!" Deena shouted and started towards the cars parked in the yard. She stopped cold at the bottom of the porch stairs.

Piled on the roof of the pearl white Caddilac Tad's parents had bought him for his sixteenth birthday where Wes' hacked and mangled torso and limbs. His head was placed as a macabre hood ornament. Scrawled in his blood on the windshield was a message.

I TOLD
YOU SO

Jason knew the message was for him. He and Tammy looked at one another. They'd expected to be able to get ahead of her dad, to beat him at his own game. That wasn't happening. They were in way over their heads.

Again, it was Deena who broke the silence.

"I can't do this!" She ran towards the dirt drive. "I've got to get out of here!"

Just before she reached the edge of the overgrown grass, a figure in ill-fitting overalls and a wide-brimmed straw hat sprang up from his hiding place in the knee-high weeds and, without pause, swung the claw end of a hammer at Deena's head. The tool lodged in her skull at the temple and she dropped to her knees. Her death was instant, so there was no fight other than the last twitches of her nervous system when the assailant roughly turned her body to face Tammy and Jason. The hammer jutted awkwardly from the side of her head. Without a word the man pried at the hammer's handle. The front of Deena's skull made a wet crunching noise and the hammer forced it to break free and tear through the skin of her forehead. A torrent of blood poured from her exposed brain cavity.

"Hi, darling, it's been a while. Daddy's come back for you," the man growled as he dropped Deena's corpse. "Now come give your old man a hug."

"Run!" Jason commanded, and the teenage couple bolted back towards the house.

He stopped abruptly before stepping onto the rotting bottom step leading up to the porch.

"I get it now. I know how to beat him."
"What? How?"

Jason grabbed the modified bat he'd hidden.

"Do you trust me?"

"Of course."

"I'm going after him with this bat, just to distract him. I need you to grab Wes' arms off the car and meet me in the barn."

"What!?" Tammy couldn't believe what she'd just heard come from his mouth. As far as she was concerned their future involved marriage, children, and growing old together. She'd never thought she'd hear something so macabre and insane come from Jason.

"You have to trust me. I'll explain in the barn. Don't let Andrew know you're there, just hide."

Her homicidal father had begun to walk towards them—hammer in hand—with a slow, menacing confidence.

"Okay. Go at him."

The escaped murderer didn't expect the bat-wielding teen to come at him. Capitalizing on having caught him off guard, Jason screamed as he swung the bat and lodged the protruding nails into the older man's knee. As soon as Jason had charged her dad, she started towards the car. Just as she took one of Wes' severed arms in each hand, she heard the squelch of cartilage and bone from the impact of Jason's bat.

"Tammy, go!" He yelled.

She rounded the house and headed towards the weathered barn. Jason, unable to dislodge his weapon before the killer gained his wits enough to swing the hammer at him, ran into the house empty handed. Inside the front door, he picked up his backpack from where he'd dropped it when they'd heard Linnea scream earlier and continued up the stairs.

Upon reaching the bedroom where two of his classmates lay dead, he retrieved his hunting knife from the schoolbag and set to work. Time was working against him, so his labor was quick and sloppy. After a couple minutes, though, he had what he needed and flew back down the stairs. As he expected, Tammy's dad was gone. If his theory was correct, Tammy would be saved for last. Andrew would be the next target, followed by Jason himself—probably dispatched directly in front of Tammy.

He'd figured out the pattern. He'd seen this play out in countless slasher films. Since he knew the mechanics at play, he knew exactly how to stop it. With a burst of heroic confidence surging through his veins, he jogged towards Deena's corpse. To his surprise, he found his bat on the ground where his injured prey had been minutes prior. Bits of meat and cartilage clung to the nails, and a trail of blood led around the back of the house. He picked up the bat after collecting what he needed from Deena, and then he set off towards the barn.

Jason didn't see Tammy's father on his way to the barn, but he knew the man was injured and moving slowly. He was assured he'd get there first.

The barn door was open, and the only light came from a single antique oil lantern hanging from a support post. Andrew was seated below it, eyes closed, swaying gently and enjoying the psilocybin journey he was on. If Andrew was still alive, so was Tammy. The clock was running out, though. He moved quickly towards his schoolmate and once he was within range he swung the bat with all his might.

Andrew's face exploded and sent blood, teeth, and bone shrapnel across the dirt floor. Jason held what was left of the stoner's head on the ground with his sneaker and dislodged the spiked end of the bat from his face.

"Jason! What the fuck are you doing?" Tammy screamed as she leapt from her hiding spot behind a rust-covered tractor.

Jason ignored her and swung again to ensure Andrew was dead.

"I figured it out. Trust me. I had to do this."

Tammy stopped several yards from him, her dreams of marriage and raising a family shattered.

"What are you talking about, Jason?"

"I need those arms," he dodged the question as he unzipped his backpack. Turning it upside-down, he emptied its contents with a wet plop. Tammy shrieked when her brain registered that the bloody pile on the ground was human skin.

"Jason," her voice was tentative, "What is going on?"

Without bothering to look at her, Jason picked up the skin of Tad's torso from the heap. It had been hastily cut and skinned from the corpse, but the intent was obvious—Jason had fashioned a vest of human skin. He slipped one arm through the hole where Tad's appendage had once been.

"These killers, the ones that go after partying teenagers like us, they always have a method and they never stop until they're killed for good," he finished putting on his skin vest and continued speaking as he reached for the next from the pile, "They go after us one by one. The jock, the cheerleader, the nerd. We all fit some mold. We always get knocked off one by one."

He'd finished clothing himself in Deena's torso, layered on top of Tad's. The dark nipples on her small chest resembled decorative buttons. He picked Linnea's bloody skin off the ground. The hook had torn up her back, so he'd left the skin across her sternum intact.

"We can't fight him by ourselves. Not me, not you. But you know what never happens?"

"What?" Tammy asked apprehensively.

"We never team up. He can beat us if he has us alone, maybe two at a time if we're distracted with sex or drugs. But he can't take us all at once."

Linnea's corpse fit him like a smock, her ample breasts streaked with blood hanging oddly from his frame.

"So, what is all this? And why Andrew?"

"It's battle armor. I needed Andrew's essence," he answered in a matter-of-fact way that made Tammy recoil. He knelt and set to slicing at the skin of the dead druggie's forearm.

"His essence? What are you talking about?"

Jason continued working as he explained. "We all have a quality about us, something that makes us who we are. Like I said before: jock, stoner, slut, nerd... whatever. Alone, we can't take him. I'm combining it all. This armor brings all that together. I'll be like an entire army. I'll take him out so he can't kill anyone else."

He removed the sleeve of Andrew's forearm skin from the muscle it had been attached to. He slid it on to his own arm, the mixture of his peers' blood providing lubrication.

"I had to sacrifice Andrew. For the greater good. Give me one of Wes' arms."

Tammy couldn't believe that she was following through with his order. She was more incredulous at how quickly he was able to fashion a second skin-gauntlet.

"I injured him, but he's still out there. Waiting for us. Andrew would have been his next. Then me. He'd have killed me in front of you, then come after you. You're his final girl."

"His what?"

"His ultimate target. The one he really wants. Don't you see, he has to kill everyone else off so we can't team up. Then he gets you all alone. The final girl's the only one with a real chance at beating him alone, but she can never really kill him."

Tammy resolved to play along. He'd lost his mind, she was sure of that, but he was still trying to protect her.

"Now you don't have to face him. I can take him out for good."

He stood before her, the tattered and bloody skin of their peers hanging on his body, his spiked bat in hand.

"Okay, then," she said, "Let's go end this."

Tammy closed the distance to her deranged boyfriend, picked the hunting knife up from a pool of blood at his feet, and leaned in to kiss him. Before she could, she giggled.

"You wanted to get in my pants, but you got into everyone else's skin instead."

"Oh no," Jason's voice was just above a whisper.

"What?"

"I need a virgin. The final girl's always a virgin. That's where the power is." The realization hit him like Wes' cup check earlier in the night. For his plan to work, the armer needed a virgin component or it wouldn't work at all. They'd both die anyway. Weighing his options, he decided that alive and single was better than dead. Plus, if he succeeded he'd be a local hero. Hero's get girls, right?

"Tammy, I love you," he brought the bat back and readied himself to swing, "I'm so sorry."

"I'm not a virgin!"

"What?" Jason paused, bat still cocked behind him.

"I was sleeping around at my old school. Dad found out and didn't want a whore for a daughter. Mom defended me, so he killed her. He wouldn't have a feminist tramp for a wife."

"That means-"

Before he could finish his sentence, Tammy swung her arm in an arc between them. The blade of the knife cut cleanly through Jason's neck, and a new wave of crimson cascaded over the skin armor. The bat fell from his hand as his body dropped to the ground. He tried to speak but nothing but a choked gurgle came from the widening gash as blood filled his trachea.

"That means you were going to kill me you crazy fuck. I'm the slut, and you're dying a virgin."

She raised her foot and stomped as hard as she could on Jason's crotch, forcing a geyser of red from his throat and the last remnants of life from his body.

"Tamara!" A gruff voice yelled from outside the barn. "You'd better come when I call you, young lady!"

"Coming, father," Tammy muttered as she knelt and began working the knife further around Jason's neck.

Minutes later, she emerged from the barn.

The old man's head cocked to the side. Something didn't look right about his daughter. In the moonlight he could make out naked breasts swaying as she walked towards him, but they sat unevenly and glistened with blood. And her face. Something was wrong with her face.

Tammy walked towards him calmly, hands at her sides. Once she was close enough her father understood why he didn't recognize her face.

It wasn't hers.

Working with Jason's own theory, she'd quickly carved away his face and scalp to wear as a mask—the final piece of armor. The drying blood did well as an adhesive, and the hanging, lifeless facial features hid her coy smile underneath.

She placidly walked directly to her father.

"Tamara you've been a filthy whore, and I can't have that. Your mother filled your head with feminist garbage, and she had to pay. The Lord doesn't like rebellious, promiscuous women. What do you have to say for yourself?"

Tammy dropped to her knees before him.

"Maybe I should pray?"

"That's a good girl. Ask the Lord to forgive you," he growled as he rose the hammer above his head.

Tammy retrieved the hunting knife from between the layers of skin she wore and clutched it, blade up, with both hands.

"Tamara, the Lord forgives those who repent," his raspy voice continued, "I don't."

Before he could act any further, Tammy jammed the steel blade into his stomach with all her might. Releasing his weapon, he doubled over and clutched his abdomen.

Tammy jumped to her feet and snatched the hammer up.

"Neither do I," she sneered from beneath Jason's face and embedded the claw end of the hammer in his left eye socket.

When she pulled it out the goopy liquid of his burst eye ran down his face as viscous tears. She raised the hammer over her head.

"This is for mom, you horrible fuck."

She brought the hammer down onto the top of his head, breaking his skull and forcing bone fragments into his brain. His body seized and dropped with a dull thump.

She stood over him in silence for several minutes, Linnea's breasts heaving with her labored breathing. Finally, she took her Jason mask off, and turned it towards her.

"Loverboy, I need to borrow your car."

She tossed the dead face to the side carelessly and ventured back towards the barn to retrieve the keys from her ex-boyfriend's jeans.

At the entrance to the barn, silhouetted by the lamplight, she mused to herself, "I guess this is where they roll the credits."

The Sleepover V

The tape hit the end and began to rewind. The boys sat in stunned silence in the dark while the tape whirred in the VCR. The unsettled feelings they'd felt all night hadn't subsided with the end of the last movie but instead brought a deeper sense of foreboding. Sean reached over and switched on the lamp. The room didn't seem out of place. Pizza boxes and empty soda cans littered the carpet in front of the television, and as the boys looked back and forth at each other, neither could form the words to express how they thought.

"I think we should get on our bikes first thing in the morning and get these movies back. I don't plan on spreading the word about that place either," Brent spoke up.

"I agree, and I'm ready to call it a night," Dillon added.

Jack sat in silence for a moment longer. "Do you think we're living in one of the movies we love so much? I mean, nothing about tonight makes any sense unless it's a plot to a horror movie."

"Yeah, let's go to bed and get rid of those fucking tapes first thing; I don't like the way they're making me feel. I did like the twist in *Final Girl,* though," Sean said. He stretched out on the couch and put his hands behind his head. "We'll look back in the morning and laugh about how big of wussies we're acting like."

Brent got on the floor and climbed around by the television. He reached around the wall until he found the outlet and unplugged the TV and VCR. The TV popped loudly, and the VCR gave a wailing whir before falling silent.

"The fuck you do that for?" Dillon asked.

"I don't trust this shit," Brent replied.

"Should we put the tapes outside?" Sean asked.

Jack picked the tapes up and sat them next to the stairs. "No, we should be fine."

"Yeah, fine," Sean whispered as the boys faded off to sleep.

30 Years Later

Sean stood in front of the abandoned building where their nightmare started. The boys awoke before dawn that Sunday morning so long ago and pedaled as fast as possible back to Employee Picks to return the VHS tapes. They rode in silence as each one pondered the dreams and nightmares they experienced during their troubled slumber.

Nothing was ever the same for them again after that night.

The sun was setting in the west, and the night felt exactly like it did the evening Sean and his friends rented the four cursed movies from Employee Picks. Now, a thick coating of dirt and grime covered the windows, and Sean couldn't see anything inside. He rubbed the glass with his sleeve, but he couldn't clean enough filth off to see inside the store.

"I can't believe it was gone the next day," Sean muttered.

When they arrived, they found Employee Picks had vanished. The storefront gave no indication the rental place had ever existed. Sean vaguely remembered the terror they felt at being saddled with the movies for the rest of their lives, but he chalked it up to the scared delusions of teenage boys.

He knew better now.

Time passed, and like most childhood friends, the four slowly faded away. Brent was the first to go. His family pulled up stakes and headed to Florida. He wrote to the others occasionally, but the letters became fewer and fewer until they eventually stopped. Sean wondered if they had cell phones if they'd been able to keep in touch, but he doubted it. The night they watched the movies changed the dynamic in the group. So, when he received word of Brent's suicide, he wasn't shocked. The bizarre taxidermy collection Brent left behind didn't surprise him either.

Dillon went next. His family ended up out in Nevada. Sean never had any contact with Dillon again until a few days ago. Dillon called from Death Row and asked Sean to forgive him. In his heart, he forgave Dillon, but the families of his victims would never give him the same benefit. Ten dead and eaten had doomed Dillon to the chair. He blocked it all out from his mind during the trial because he always wondered what had caused his old friend to snap.

He had an idea, but he sat around and waited for the news of Jack to find him. The news of all his friend's misfortunes always had a way of finding him, and when it did, it was like losing a piece of his soul.

Finally, while scrolling through an internet chatroom, a man claimed to have watched his neighbor carve up his face with shards from a broken mirror. He knew he'd found Jack. The man must have been trying to see what was inside himself, and he found himself to be red all over. The man died, and Sean looked at the date. Brent's suicide, Dillon's execution, and Jack's death all happened on the same day.

Sean laughed in front of the empty store. He was the final one. When they watched the movies in Sean's backpack, they didn't believe in ghosts and demons. Now, Sean knew they were real. All four of them fought with their demons and lost their entire lives. He'd done his fair share of bad shit in his life. The last twenty-four hours found him trying not to take on the character flaw of the final girl from his movie, but the bum he ran across changed that.

The man's blood felt good, splashing on his skin. Sean got excited when the bum's eyes closed and his soul left his body. He was the final one for a reason, and something drew him back to the store. His whole life, he'd tried to leave the town, but something always held him back.

He was the Final Boy.

Inside the empty store, the lights came on, and the 'Open' sign lit up. Sean smiled as he entered Employee Picks, knowing he had a job to do for eternity because the store was open for business again.

About The Authors

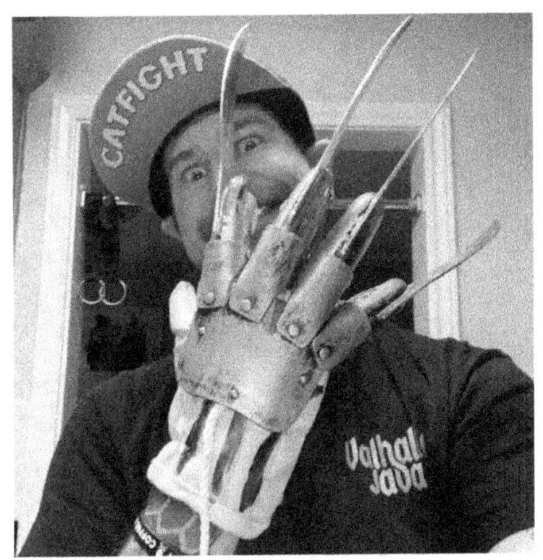

About Sean

Sean Cochrane is a lifelong fan of all things evil and macabre. He lives in Round Rock, Texas with his wife and three children. When not writing he subsists on a steady diet of horror, heavy metal, punk rock, and coffee.

Sean is also featured in Disquieted: A Brief Horror Collection.

About Brent

Brent Abell resides in Southern Indiana with his wife and Drake the Puggle. Brent enjoys anything horror related. In his writing career, he's had stories featured in over 30 publications from multiple presses. His books Southern Devils, Southern Devils: Reconstruction of the Dead, In Memoriam, The Calling, Dying Days: Death Sentence, Death Inc., and Wicked Tales for Wicked People are available now. He is also a co-author of the horror-comedy Hellmouth series. Currently he is working on a multitude of projects. You can hang out with him at http://brentabell.com for some rum and a good cigar.

About Dillon

Dillon Brown is the owner and creator of Horror Nerd Productions, an independent film company that showcases local talent on tiny budgets. Along with writing and directing his own films, Dillon is also the author of three published novellas. He currently lives in Reno, Nevada with his wife and step-son.

About Jack

Jack Wallen is what happens when a Gen Xer mind-melds with present day snark. Jack is a seeker of truth and a writer of words with a quantum mechanical pencil and a disjointed beat of sound and soul. Although he resides in the unlikely city of Louisville, Kentucky, Jack likes to think of himself more as an interplanetary traveler, on the lookout for the Satellite of Love ad a perpetual movie sign... or so he tells the reflection in the mirror (sometimes in 3rd person). Jack is the author of numerous tales of dark twisty fiction including the I Zombie series, the Reapers and the fEaR series (published by Devil Dog Press), the Suicide series, the Klockwerk Movement, the Fringe Killer series, Shero, The Nameless Saga, and much more.

BE KIND
REWIND